C
A FLEE

Silhouette Desire

Originally Published by Silhouette Books
a division of
Harlequin Enterprises Ltd.

*First published in Great Britain in 1993
by Silhouette Books, Eton House, 18-24 Paradise Road,
Richmond, Surrey TW9 1SR*

© Carla Bracale 1993

*Silhouette, Silhouette Desire and Colophon are
Trade Marks of Harlequin Enterprises B.V.*

ISBN 0 373 59013 X

22-9310

Made and printed in Great Britain

CARLA CASSIDY

has been a cheerleader for the Kansas City Chiefs football team and traveled the East Coast as a singer and
dancer in a band, but the greatest pleasure she's had is in
creating romance and happiness for readers.

One

"I've got an assignment for you," Walter Cummings said, leaning back in the chair behind the desk.

Cliff Marchelli leaned forward, eyeing the captain of the Kansas City Police Department eagerly. "What kind of assignment?"

"Surveillance." Walt winced, apparently waiting for the explosion of anger he knew would come.

Cliff didn't disappoint him. He swept his hand irritably through his dark, unruly hair, then jumped out of his chair and began to pace the confines of the small office. "Damn it, Walt, you know how much I hate surveillance. Why can't Charlie or one of the other guys take the assignment? Give me something with some action?"

"Cliff, please sit down," Walt said patiently. "And settle down or your ulcers are going to flare up again."

"Working surveillance is what gave me ulcers," Cliff said dryly, refolding his lanky length back into the chair.

"Cliff, you've been on a merry-go-round of cases for the past two years. Hell, man, I can't even remember the last time you had a decent vacation."

"I don't need a vacation," Cliff said tersely. He saw the implacable expression on Walt's face and sighed resignedly. "So, what's going down?"

"Word out on the streets is that a major buy is coming down in the next two weeks."

"What's the location?" Cliff asked.

"A warehouse in the northeast section. We've been looking for a place to hole up in and yesterday we found the perfect place, an apartment building directly across from the warehouse. The apartment on the second floor has a window that looks directly into the warehouse. There's only one small catch...." Walt paused, a pained expression on his face. "The apartment is occupied."

"Walt, what are you trying to do to me?" Cliff felt his stomach rumbling in protest.

The chief chuckled. "Cliff, you've wrestled with drug-crazed junkies and busted up a mob-connected escort service. Surely you can get the cooperation of a little old lady and her granddaughter."

"A little old lady..." Cliff stared at him in consternation. "Walt..."

Walt held up his hands to still Cliff's protests. "I know it's not the best of circumstances, but it's all we've got. The apartment is perfect." Walt leaned over the top of the desk. "Look, Cliff, I know it's irregular, but I've got my behind in the proverbial sling. The mayor is breathing down my back on this particular bust. Besides, it should only be for the next two weeks and you can assure the two women there's no danger involved."

"When do I start?"

"Tonight if you can get it set up this afternoon. We ran a quick check on the two women." Walt shuffled papers on his desk, finding the one he sought and reading from it. "The granddaughter is Edith Turner. She's living in the apartment to care for her grandmother. They both seem to be upstanding citizens and I'm sure they'll be most accommodating in helping us out. We want the warehouse observed from 6:00 p.m. to 7:00 a.m. Our inside sources say sometime between those hours the buy will be made." For the next few minutes Walt went over all the particulars of the case with Cliff. "Any questions?" he asked when they were finished.

Cliff shook his head and stood.

"Oh, one more thing, Cliff." Walt also stood. "I'll keep in touch, and remember, it's good PR to be pleasant to the civilians. And before you set things up with them, get a haircut." Walt's voice followed Cliff out into the hallway of the metro police department building.

"Yeah, right," Cliff muttered to himself, knowing he would do no such thing. He wasn't about to get a haircut just to impress a sick old woman and her nursemaid granddaughter. Edith Turner... he could just imagine what a prize she was. A no-nonsense woman who was devoting her life to taking care of a sick grandmother. His mind immediately conjured up a picture of a tall, muscular woman, her hair cut militantly short. "She probably wears support hose and has the personality of a rock," he mumbled, leaving the police station and going out into the warmth of the early-autumn sunshine. Not that he cared what this Edith Turner looked like. All he wanted from her was the use of the window of her apartment.

Cliff got into his car, slamming the door more forcefully than necessary. Damn, he hated surveillance, especially when the surveillance was on a building rather than a person. A building couldn't get up and walk away, couldn't break the monotony of the game. As far as Cliff was concerned, there was nothing worse than the boredom of sitting long into the night with only inner thoughts to provide company. Inner thoughts, stale coffee and junk food, he added grimly. He started the car with a grimace. He wasn't sure what was worse, the expectation of being alone with his own thoughts or the thought of having to be pleasant to an old maid named Edith. If he was lucky, Edith Turner would go to bed with the sun about seven-thirty, leaving him to his own devices for the long, boring night of watching the warehouse.

Edie Turner quickly closed the bedroom door and leaned against it tiredly. Finally her grandmother had fallen asleep. She'd been so restless the night before and this morning hadn't been much better. It wasn't until Edie had fed her lunch that the elderly woman had fallen into slumber.

She eyed the couch longingly. There was nothing she'd like more than a little catnap, but a stack of tapes and the Dictaphone on the kitchen table sat in silent accusation, reminding her that she had neglected her work long enough. She looked at her wristwatch, noting that it was only a few minutes after two o'clock. She could work for a couple of hours before she began fixing supper.

She had just sat down at her word processor and put the earphones of the Dictaphone into her ears when the doorbell rang. She shot a worried look at the closed bedroom door, hoping the loud buzzer hadn't awakened Nanny. Yanking the earphones out of her ears, she hurried to the door. Making sure the chain guard was fastened, she opened the door the four inches the chain would allow and peered out.

Her first thought was that one of the lowlifes who had recently begun to frequent the area had mistaken her apartment for another. The man standing on the other side of her door certainly looked like a lowlife. A shock of dark, curly hair covered his head, falling over his eyes and tumbling down on his forehead to meet his thick, dark eyebrows. His nose was slightly crooked, as if it had been broken and never reset properly. His lips were thin and taut, set in what looked to be grim determination. He was dressed in a sweatshirt that did nothing to hide his broad shoulders, and the worn jeans he had on caressed the contours of his legs like a familiar lover. Very attractive, in a dangerous sort of way, her mind instantly computed. But definitely an unsavory character.

"Yes?" she asked coolly.

"Edith Turner?" he inquired.

Edie looked at him in surprise. "Yes, I'm Edith Turner." She noticed his eyes for the first time—dark eyes that radiated nothing of his soul.

"I'm Cliff Marchelli from the police department," he began.

"Right, and I'm Zsa Zsa Gabor." Edie slammed the door shut in his face. If that man was a police officer then she was the man in the moon. More likely he was one of the transients the area attracted who'd heard that Edie Turner was a soft touch when it came to a handout of food. This certainly wasn't the first incredible story she'd heard for a handout.

Last month in the city market she'd been confronted by a transient who'd explained to her that he was an ambassador of goodwill from the planet of Zoron, and all he needed to get established on earth was enough money to buy a little ripple. She smiled, then thought again of the man on the other side of the door. Maybe he really was a cop. She opened the door again, squeaking with surprise as his hand snaked through the opening.

"Here, Zsa Zsa, read this," his deep voice said through the door. He held out a wallet, flipped open to display a badge and an ID card.

Edie took the wallet and studied the badge. It looked real enough, but that was no guarantee. His picture was on the ID card, along with his name and precinct number. Still, Edie was smart enough to be wary. Anyone could obtain a fake ID.

"Look, call the precinct and ask for Walt Cummings. He's my chief." He sighed impatiently.

"I'll just do that," Edie replied, getting her phone book and reaching for the phone.

Cliff leaned against the door, listening to the sound of the phone being dialed. Edith Turner was not at all what he'd been expecting. For one thing, she wasn't tall and thin as he'd imagined. From the brief glimpse he had gotten of her, she barely came up to his shoulders. Her hair hadn't been cut militantly short, rather it had been a careless braid of chestnut color. He leaned closer to the door as he heard her voice apparently speaking over the telephone.

"I have a man at my door who claims to be an officer, and I just thought it would be prudent to check it out with you. Yes, he looks...uh...rather seedy."

Cliff bristled at her description and looked down at himself. He didn't look seedy...well, maybe just a little.... Maybe he should have gotten the haircut Walt had suggested, and he probably should have shaved that morning. He pressed more tightly against the door, listening to the conversation going on. "Yes, that's right. Yes, I see. Thank you. I'll be in touch."

Before Cliff had an opportunity to move away from the door, she pulled it open, causing him to stumble inside. He caught his balance before he careened into the small oak dining table, a ruddy color suffusing his face.

"Come in, Mr. Marchelli," she said, holding out his wallet to him.

He took the wallet and shoved it into his back pocket. "Uh, could we sit down?" he asked, looking around at the dainty, feminine furnishings. He regretted the suggestion almost immediately. The sofa was high-backed with little wooden legs that looked as if they would splinter under any weight over a hundred pounds. The two chairs gave the same sort of impression.

"Of course." She gestured to the sofa, then seeing his unease she smiled. "I promise, it's much more durable than it looks."

Cliff nodded curtly, then eased himself carefully down on the sofa, sighing with relief when the legs didn't shatter and fling him onto the floor.

For a moment he sat there, looking around the place where, if things worked out, he would be spending the next two weeks of his life. The room where they sat was fairly good sized, a living room and kitchen combination. The kitchen appliances were against the far wall, and on the opposite wall was the window that overlooked the warehouse.

What struck him most was the fact that the apartment seemed to be filled with life. Green plants hung in the window, their foliage draping down toward a window seat filled with decorative throw pillows. Copper utensils and pots hung on the wall above the stove, their tarnished bottoms reflecting everyday usage. The antique furniture was highly polished, the gleaming surfaces showing loving attention. The walls were covered with pictures, testimony to a lifetime of friends and family. Cliff was disconcerted by the air of intimacy the place emitted, so different from his own functional, impersonal apartment.

"Did you come here to admire the decor or is there another purpose for this visit?" Edie asked dryly, not missing the way his dark eyes inventoried every corner of the room. For some reason his cool, appraising survey made her feel slightly violated, as if he had peeked into her underwear drawer and knew the color of her panties.

Cliff heard the ill-concealed aggravation in her voice and looked at her, surprised to find himself even more disconcerted by the mere act of gazing at her. She was so different than what he had expected. She was so attractive, with her burnished hair pulled away from her heart-shaped face to fully expose the delicate features. Although she was small, she was perfectly proportioned. The tight jeans she wore did nothing to hide the rounded curves of her hips, and pert breasts pushed against the pale blue material of her clinging blouse. She was attractive enough to spark the memory of an emotion he had denied himself for a long time. He sat up straighter on the sofa, perversely irritated with her for not fitting into his preconceived mold of staid nursemaid.

"The police department needs your help," Cliff began, noticing for the first time the brown of her eyes, the color of a cup of coffee with a touch of cream.

"My help?" She looked at him curiously.

He nodded, averting his gaze from her, finding it easier to talk to her if he wasn't looking at her. He quickly explained the situation to her. "I'll only be here at night and your life should continue pretty normally,'' he finished.

Edie smiled subconsciously at this. Her life hadn't been what was considered normal for the past year, not since Nanny had gotten ill. ''What exactly would this entail?''

''I'll be here every evening around six o'clock, and I'll sit in front of that window with some video equipment until seven in the morning. Most of my work will take place while you're sleeping. What we would require of you is your silence concerning our presence here and your interior lights kept off during the hours of surveillance.'' Cliff's jaw tightened reflexively. Once again he found himself discomfited by her as a sudden, dangerous curiosity flitted through his mind. Did she wear nightgowns to bed? Soft, filmy things that would lightly caress her feminine curves?

Damn her for being so attractive. He cleared his throat, consciously focusing his mind on his purpose for being here. ''I can guarantee you there is no danger and I'll disrupt your routine as little as possible. Can we count on your cooperation?''

She hesitated a moment, then nodded. ''When will you start?''

''Tonight at six.''

''Then I guess it's settled. I'll see you tonight at six.''

He nodded and stood, then walked to the door. ''If we're both very lucky, this bust will go down in the next two weeks and you'll see the back end of me.'' With these words he left the apartment.

''Terrific,'' Edie muttered, closing the door and re-locking it. That man made Dirty Harry look positively benign. Not only did he need a haircut and shave, he could use a class on public relations, as well.

Oh, well, it was only for two weeks, and it would be nice to know she was contributing in some small way to cleaning up the neighborhood. As long as Cliff did what he was supposed to do, for two weeks she could pretend he was part of the furniture. She sat back down at the table, put the Dictaphone earplugs back into her ears and turned on the machine.

As Cliff drove back toward the Turner apartment at five-thirty that evening, he silently cursed Walt for handing him this particular assignment.

After leaving the Turner apartment earlier in the day, he'd headed home, intent on getting some sleep before he had to return for his all-night observation. He'd gotten undressed and crawled into bed, but sleep had been elusive. Instead, he'd found his mind plagued with torturous thoughts of the past. Edith Turner's coffee-colored eyes had evoked memories of another pair of brown eyes—Catherine's eyes.

He'd pulled himself out of bed and headed straight to the gym, where two hours of physical exertion had effectively banished thoughts of the past. Unfortunately, nothing had successfully lightened his foul mood. If anything, his hostility had grown more intense, and most of it was focused on Edith Turner. It was her fault that he'd thought about Catherine. But more than that, for a brief moment while he had been sitting in her apartment, Edith Turner had caused a brief flare of desire to lick at his soul. The emotion had been an unwelcome intruder from the past.

Cliff shook his head and focused on his surroundings as he drove into the northeast area of Kansas City.
As he drove down the narrow streets, he found himself thinking what a shame it was that this part of the
city had been allowed to decay and erode with the
passing of time. Most of the stately old buildings had
either been abandoned or converted into warehouses.

"What in the hell are Edith Turner and her grandmother doing living in this area?" he murmured,
parking his car on the street next to the apartment
building. He frowned with aggravation and got out of
the car. He didn't care if Edith Turner lived on the
moon. All he wanted to do was get this surveillance
job over with, and move on to his next assignment.

He grabbed two duffel bags from the back seat of
the car, locked the automobile, then headed for the
apartment. The apartment building itself wasn't in bad
shape. It was a three-story red brick, with two apartments on each floor. The woodwork of the hallway
was in good shape, and the walls looked freshly
painted. As he walked up the stairs to the second floor,
his stomach rumbled as the smell of homemade Italian tomato sauce wafted in the air. He sighed, thinking of the two chili dogs that nestled in one of the
duffel bags. Between the stress of doing this unwanted job and his penchant for convenience foods,
he'd be swallowing antacids by the handful. He sighed
again and knocked on the Turner apartment door. His
stress level immediately rose as she opened the door
and greeted him.

"Come in, Mr. Marchelli."

Cliff grabbed his two duffel bags and entered the apartment. "You might as well call me Cliff," he grunted, setting the bags down by the window.

"And you can call me Edie," she returned.

Edie . . . yes, that suited her much more than Edith, he thought as he bent over and began removing items from one of the duffel bags. He concentrated on putting together the tripod and video equipment, consciously ignoring her presence near him. At least she'd changed out of the tight jeans and blouse she'd been wearing earlier. She was now wearing a loose, floor-length caftan that covered her from neck to feet.

He felt himself beginning to relax as he occupied himself with the task of getting prepared for the long night ahead. As long as he didn't look at her, he could almost pretend she wasn't here. Now if only she would move far enough away from him so he couldn't smell the floral scent that seemed to emanate from her.

When he'd finished unpacking the video equipment he turned to the second duffel bag and pulled out his police radio, a notepad, the bag containing his chili dogs, binoculars and a thermos of coffee.

"What's the camera for?" she asked curiously.

Cliff grimaced. It would be difficult to pretend she wasn't here if she spoke to him. "To record the warehouse if I have to leave the window for any amount of time. Then when I return I can play back the video and see if anything has happened." He didn't look at her, and his voice was filled with a tinge of impatience.

"Oh, so it's sort of like a partner," Edie exclaimed. She smiled humorlessly. "Only I'll bet it doesn't complain about overtime or need coffee breaks.''

"Yeah, and it doesn't indulge in idle chatter,'' he returned.

"Well, excuse me,'' Edie said glacially. She stomped across the room and busied herself filling a teakettle of water, then placed it on the stove.

He breathed a sigh of relief. Good, now maybe she understood that he was here to do a job. No personal involvements, no friendly pleasantries—just his job. He set the camera on the tripod, then focused it out the window, frowning as he realized the hanging foliage from the plants obscured his view. "Could I move one of these plants?'' he asked.

"I'll do it,'' Edie muttered, thinking his hostility would probably kill the begonia. She stood up on the window seat and reached up to remove the plant hanger from the hook where it had been suspended. She immediately grunted beneath the weight of the huge plant and grabbed for the pot. Cliff, seeing her distress and realizing the plant was too heavy for her to manage alone, also grabbed for the pot. Suddenly his hands were trapped against her body, caught between the ceramic surface of the colorful pot and the warm softness of her breasts. Edie, too, found her hands trapped between the pot and Cliff's hard chest. Neither of them could step back without the pot crashing to the floor.

"Uh...let's take it over to the table,'' Edie said shakily as he nodded his agreement, his face flushed a vivid red. As they walked across the length of the room toward the table, his knuckles moved gently across the peaks of each breast with each step they took. Edie was appalled to feel her body responding to the pressure of his touch, an erotic answering flame igniting within her.

The pot hit the table with a loud thud as they both released it at the same time. "Thanks," Edie murmured, turning toward the stove where her teakettle had begun to emit steam in a soundless whistle. She was mortified by her body's response to his accidental touch.

"No problem," he returned, going back to the window and concentrating on focusing the camera out the pane of glass. His hands shook slightly as he adjusted the focus. His body had reacted automatically and immediately to her proximity, suddenly reminding him that he was a normal man with a healthy libido that had been denied for a very long time.

"Hello? Who's there?"

Cliff jumped at the sound of an unexpected, unfamiliar voice. "Who is that?"

She flushed slightly. "My grandmother."

He frowned. He'd forgotten all about the old woman.

"Excuse me," Edie said, disappearing into the bedroom. Cliff could hear her talking soothingly, then the answering, more querulous voice of the elderly woman. The older woman's voice rose sharply and Edie came back into the room and looked at Cliff hesitantly. "I'm sorry to bother you, but could you come in and meet my grandmother? She heard your voice and won't settle down until you come in and say hello."

Cliff sighed and stood, then followed Edie into the bedroom. The first thing he saw when he entered the room was the large oak bed, and in the bed was a small, white-haired woman. She sat with all the demeanor of a queen, her blue eyes sharp and keen in the wizened face. She waved away Edie, who was plumping the pillows behind her head. "Who are you?" she demanded, plucking peevishly at the lace collar of her blue nightgown.

"I'm Cliff Marchelli," Cliff answered.

"Cliff's a friend of mine, Nanny. He came to visit for the evening," she added, shooting Cliff a look of warning. She obviously didn't want the older woman to know he was a cop.

"Come over here where I can see you better," she demanded.

Cliff took a couple of steps closer to the bed.

"That's close enough," she snapped, causing him to stop in his tracks. She eyed him warily, her bright eyes full of suspicion. She turned suddenly and looked at Edie. "I don't like him," she announced. "He's got mean, beady little eyes." She turned back and glared at Cliff, then stuck her tongue out at him.

Cliff sighed, the acid in his stomach starting to burn. This was definitely going to be the longest two weeks of his life.

Two

"Would you like me to turn on your television?" Edie asked, her tone solicitous.

"No, don't want to watch TV," Nanny replied, a small pout pursing her wrinkled lips. "I want to go for a walk."

"Okay, we'll go for a little walk," Edie agreed. "But first we need to get you dressed, and I have to change clothes."

Nanny started to rise out of the bed, then glared at Cliff once again. "Go on, get on out of here. I know you're just hanging around here hoping you'll get a glimpse of my luscious limbs."

Cliff fled the room, a scarlet flush on his face. He grabbed one of the wooden chairs from the dining table and pulled it up in front of the window. Sitting down, he grabbed his bottle of antacid tablets and popped two into his mouth. "I'm going to kill you, Walt," he muttered under his breath. *An attractive granddaughter who thinks I'm seedy, and a grandmother who thinks I want her body—how can this job get any worse?* He crunched into the tablets, hoping the chalky medicine would relieve the burning sensation in the pit of his stomach.

He didn't turn when the door to the bedroom opened and the two women walked out. He studiously ignored both of them, staring out the window.

"What are you, some sort of Peeping Tom?" Nanny said from behind him. Cliff didn't answer, unsure how Edie wanted to handle the presence of him and his video equipment in the apartment. "I knew you were a pervert when I first saw you." Without warning she smacked him on the back of his head.

"Hey," Cliff protested, turning around and rubbing the area where she had struck.

"Nanny, that wasn't nice at all." Edie's voice was stern and a light blush stained her cheeks as she smiled apologetically at Cliff. Nanny smiled, too, the self-satisfied smile of a child caught doing something wrong and getting away with it. "Come on, let's go for our walk." Edie led her grandmother out the apartment door.

Cliff watched them go, not about to turn his back on Nanny and be ambushed again. He didn't relax until the door closed firmly behind them, then he sighed and leaned back in his chair. Walt had said an ill, elderly woman. He'd neglected to mention the fact that she had the personality characteristics of a pit bull. He rubbed the back of his head again. She hadn't hurt him, but she had certainly managed to surprise him.

He leaned forward in the chair, looking out the window to the sidewalk directly below. He immediately caught sight of Edie and Nanny walking down the sidewalk, the younger woman's steps small and measured to allow for her grandmother's snail-like pace. As Cliff watched, Edie attempted to take her grandmother's arm, but the old woman thwarted her efforts by batting Edie's hands away. A small smile lifted one corner of his mouth. He wasn't sure who was feistier, the old woman or the younger one who took care of her. It was the younger one who captured his gaze once again.

Twilight was falling outside, painting the world in golden hues. A shaft of waning sunlight danced in Edie's burnished hair, as if enjoying one last moment of freedom before being pulled into the encroaching darkness of night. His gaze moved downward, watching her long braid as it bounced across her slender back with each step she took. He couldn't help but notice the way the worn jeans she was wearing molded to her shapely derriere. Disconcerted by the direction in which his thoughts were going, he tore his gaze away from the two figures.

He looked around the interior of the apartment once again, knowing with a cop's instinct that nothing would happen at the warehouse as long as daylight reigned outside.

He got up off the chair, drawn to the wall that displayed the array of photographs. The center photo was an old black-and-white picture of a bride and groom. A youthful Nanny? She'd probably hog-tied the poor man to get him to the altar, he thought wryly.

Surrounding the wedding pictures were other photos, including several of Edith Turner at various stages in her life. He could almost chronicle the passing of years by the length of her braid. There was a school picture of her, flashing a gap-toothed grin, her braid curling around her neck and just barely touching the top of her shoulder. A graduation picture, her face glowing with expectation, the ever-present braid twisted around her head like a crown.

His eyes lingered on a photo of her in a huge Kansas University T-shirt. The large shirt did nothing to conceal her shapeliness, and the chestnut braid fell over her shoulder and curled around one rounded breast. His hands began to tingle, as if on their own volition, remembering the brief contact with her warm, soft breasts.

What was he doing standing here staring at pictures of people he didn't know, thinking about an accidental brush against a woman he cared nothing about? He threw himself back into his chair in front of the window and grabbed the sack containing his two chili dogs. As bad as his ulcers felt at the moment, the chili dogs certainly couldn't hurt.

Outside on the sidewalk below, Edie walked patiently beside her grandmother. Nanny's steps were slow and awkward, attesting to the poor circulation that made movement of her legs difficult.

Every evening if Nanny felt up to it they walked first down one side of the street then up the other side. Nanny enjoyed the walks and Edie felt they were good for her. If Nanny was having a very good day she would point to buildings that held memories: the small structure on the corner that used to be the Italian bakery, the empty lot where a popular restaurant once existed. This evening nothing sparked memories in Nanny's mind. She looked around the area as if she had never seen it before, hadn't lived in the very same apartment for the past fifty-eight years. Edie knew the lack of memories was directly attributable to the illness that robbed Nanny of her soul, replacing it with fragmented pieces of bewilderment, confusion and anger. Less and less often did the essence of the gentle, loving woman who'd raised Edie surface as the disease continued to gain an unalterable control.

A small smile touched her lips as she remembered the look of surprise on Cliff's face when Nanny had cuffed him on the back of his head. His dark eyes had lit with a spark of life that hadn't been present before. In that unguarded moment, with his eyes sparkling with animation, she had found him vastly appealing.

"Why'd you bring me here?" Nanny's voice intruded into her thoughts.

"We're just having a nice little walk, Nanny," Edie said, grateful to have something to take her mind away from the dark, dour policeman in her apartment.

"Why are we walking in this neighborhood? I don't like it here."

Edie took hold of her grandmother's hand and smiled gently. "Nanny, this is your neighborhood. Look, over there is your apartment building." She pointed across the street to the three-story brick building.

Nanny looked across the street at the apartments, her brow wrinkled in perplexity. "No, I don't think I live there. That place looks like a dump."

Edie smiled, but didn't try to contradict her grandmother. She knew from experience that it would do no good to refute Nanny's error. It would only serve to confuse her even more.

"Come on, let's go back home and get something to eat."

As they started to enter the apartment building they met Rose and her son coming out of the door. A soft, inward sigh escaped Edie. She adored the plump Italian woman, but in another life Edie was certain that Rose Tonnilesco had been a professional matchmaker, and for the past year she'd had her sights set on making a love match between Edie and her son, Anthony.

"Ah, Edie and Nanny." Rose's broad face beamed. "How was your walk tonight, Nanny, love?" Rose enunciated each word carefully and loudly, as if Nanny was suffering from deafness.

"Who are you?" Nanny demanded, her bright blue eyes mistrusting.

"I'm Rose, you remember. I'm your friend, Rose."

Nanny moved closer to Rose, her gaze searching the broad, olive-skinned face intently. "No, you're not. Rose is young, and you're old."

Rose cackled with laughter. "You're absolutely right, my friend. Age has a tendency of creeping up on you when you aren't looking." She smiled kindly at Nanny, then turned her attention to Edie. "Edie, you remember Anthony, I told you he was visiting for a couple of days."

Edie smiled up at the thin, dark-haired man standing next to Rose. "Of course I do. Hello, Anthony, nice to see you again." She and Anthony, at Rose's insistence, had shared a miserable evening together on a date two months before. Within fifteen minutes of being together it had been obvious to both of them that the date was a big mistake. There had been no attraction, no spark of interest. Thankfully they'd been able to admit it to each other and had spent the remainder of the evening driving around and talking until an hour Rose would think reasonable for a date to end. The result had been an enjoyable friendship.

"Hi, Edie." A shy smile curved Anthony's mouth.

"Anthony's engaged," Rose explained, looking at Edie wistfully. "Ah...I had such high hopes...." A heavy sigh puffed out her cheeks.

"Congratulations, Anthony," Edie exclaimed, happy that the shy, quiet man had found a woman he wanted to wed.

"I just hope this young woman is ready to start a family. I'd like to live long enough to see my first grandchild."

Anthony took his mother's arm firmly. "Come on, Mama. We can discuss my plans for children later. I don't want to keep Sherri waiting."

Rose rolled her brown eyes. "He used to be worried about keeping me waiting, now he's worried about keeping this Sherri person waiting." She sighed, the well-perfected, long-suffering sigh.

Edie smiled as they said their goodbyes and walked down the sidewalk. Poor Sherri would have her work cut out for her with Rose as a mother-in-law.

As she and Nanny reentered the apartment, Cliff turned from the window.

"Who's he?" Nanny immediately demanded.

"Nanny, this is Cliff, a friend of mine," Edie said, as if she hadn't introduced the two less than half an hour before.

This time it was Cliff who eyed Nanny warily. He wasn't exactly sure what to expect from the older woman, but he was ready for anything.

"Are you Bessie's boy?" Nanny asked.

"No," Cliff answered.

"Nanny, Bessie and her son don't live here anymore," Edie answered.

"What was her boy's name?"

"Johnny," Edie answered, leading her to a chair at the table. "Now, you sit here and I'll get us some supper."

"I want tacos," Nanny announced.

"Nanny, you know we don't eat tacos." Edie's statement was punctuated by the opening of the refrigerator door. "I've got some delicious eggplant casserole."

"Yuck," Nanny replied eloquently. "I want tacos."

Cliff felt a flare of empathy for her. *Yuck* was right. If given the choice between eggplant casserole and hot-spiced, crunchy tacos, he'd take the latter every time and heartburn be damned.

"This is much better for you," Edie said, and Cliff heard the sound of the microwave humming. Her answer seemed to satisfy Nanny, who didn't say any more about tacos. In fact, for the remainder of the meal Nanny didn't say another word. Edie kept up a steady stream of soothing conversation, reminding the older woman to use her fork instead of her fingers, pleasantries about acquaintances and old friends. Cliff found himself enjoying the sound of her talking. Her voice was low and melodious, reminding him of the low-toned chimes of a distant church bell.

He was silent while they ate. Darkness had fallen outside, shrouding the world in mystery except where the street lamps provided illumination. Inside his head a mystery of sorts was revealing itself. What was wrong with the old woman? It was obvious she had a mental condition of some sort. Was it merely a case of senility or something else?

Did Edie ever get a chance to get out, socialize with people her own age? Was there a special man in her life?

He sat up straighter in his chair, surprised by the alien emotion swimming around in his head. Curiosity. . . God, how long had it been since he'd been genuinely curious about anything or anyone other than his work?

He shifted his position, silently berating himself for allowing a momentary interest to enter his mind. He didn't want to know anything about Edie and her grandmother. To know somebody you ran the risk of coming to care about that person, and caring was something he had vowed he would never do again.

Immediately after eating, Edie took her grandmother into the bedroom. Almost half an hour later she returned to the living room alone.

"She's asleep," she said, coming to stand behind him. He knew she was there because he could smell her fragrance, a light floral scent he found exceedingly appealing. The fact that he could find the smell attractive irritated him. "Cliff..." She touched his shoulder lightly, jerking her hand back as his muscles knotted tensely and he turned to look at her with his dark, fathomless eyes.

"What?" The word was a sharp bark.

"I—I just wanted to apologize for Nanny's behavior earlier," she stuttered, taking a step backward, surprised by his animosity.

A tense smile touched his lips. The smile looked out of place, as if it was an expression his mouth had tried on and wasn't accustomed to wearing. "I have to admit, she packs quite a wallop," he replied.

Edie smiled. "I've never seen her hit anyone before." The smile slowly faded. "She's always been spunky and more than a little bit stubborn, but the hitting... it's just another symptom of her illness."

"What's wrong with her?" The question was out of his mouth before he had a chance to stop it.

"She has Alzheimer's disease."

Cliff frowned. "I don't know too much about it, but shouldn't she be in a hospital or a nursing home?"

Edie nodded slowly, regret furrowing her brow. "Yes, eventually I'll have to put her in a nursing-home facility. It will become too difficult for me to keep her here. But for now she still has moments when she knows who I am and where she is, and she's comforted by that. When those lucid moments no longer surface, then I'll have to make other arrangements."

A poignant smile lifted her features. It suddenly seemed important to her that he know the woman she'd grown up with, that he understand why she felt the need to care for Nanny as long as possible. "Nanny and Gramps raised me, and I guess I feel like by taking care of her now I'm repaying all the years of sacrifice they made for me."

"Where are your parents?"

"They died in a car accident when I was four years old. Nanny and Gramps are the only parents I've ever known. Gramps passed away five years ago."

Cliff felt a sudden affinity with her. He, too, knew the pain of losing loved ones. But wasn't she just setting herself for more pain by hanging on to her grandmother when the result would be another loss? He pulled himself up short, not wanting to empathize with her. He didn't want to feel anything but cold, impersonal detachment. There was safety in that.

"Look, this little sojourn into your family history has been fun, but I'm not here to research the Turner family tree. I'm here to do my job." He instantly regretted the sarcastic words when he saw the stricken look on her face, but he consciously ignored his twinge of guilt. Somehow, some way, this woman was a threat to the secure cocoon he'd built for himself over the past two years. Better she hate him, better he make her angry than risk the peace of mind he'd found in his life.

Whew, and had he made her angry. He could tell by the rigid way her shoulders were set as she stalked across the room. She didn't try to hide her fury, either. Her footsteps were heavy, thundering across the floor, belying her small stature. The dishes from the table were thrown into the sink, punctuated by under-the-breath mutterings. Cabinet doors were slammed with a vengeance.

"I know I'm not supposed to turn on lights, but could I light some candles?" Her voice was a blast of cold, arctic air. He nodded, watching as she began to light the candles that decorated the room. He wondered vaguely if the candles were some sort of a ceremonial process and she was putting a voodoo curse on him. He supposed he wouldn't worry unless she pulled out a couple of his hairs or asked to clip his fingernails.

Edie was mad, all right—madder than she could remember being in a very long time, madder than the situation warranted. Okay, so he was uncivil, but she had dealt with rude people before. She was puzzled, as well. Why was he able to get under her skin so completely? She looked over to where he was sitting, his attention focused out the window. The thing that irritated her most was that he had asked about Nanny, he'd expressed an interest, then had rebuffed her for answering him. She'd seen the flicker of curiosity in his eyes. Then, as if somebody had pushed the Off button on the television set, his eyes had reverted to blank screens.

She finished lighting the scented candles, then poured herself a glass of white wine, carried the crystal goblet over to the sofa and sat down. She kicked off her shoes, placed her feet on the coffee table and willed herself to relax. This was the time of the evening when she wound down, luxuriating in time spent doing nothing except sipping a glass of wine and smelling the pleasant mixture of fragrances coming from the flickering candles. She called it her stress-down process, when she shrugged off the worries and tensions of the day like a snake liberating itself from an old skin. But tonight, the peace of mind she'd come to expect eluded her. And it was all his fault. She shot a somber gaze at Cliff. He was like a gloomy sentry invading her space. Even with her back to him and his back to her, she could feel his presence. Like an unhappy child at a birthday party who cast a shadow of misery over the rest of the guests, Cliff's moroseness drew a dark pall over Edie.

She shifted her weight on the sofa so she was sitting sideways and looked at his back once again. His shoulders looked taut, and she could easily imagine the muscles beneath his sweatshirt knotted with tension. She felt a sudden, crazy desire to walk up behind him and let her fingers massage away the tenseness. The very thought surprised her, and frightened her just a little.

"Are you married?" The question fell out of her mouth before she was conscious of it being formulated in her mind.

He turned and looked at her, his gaze dark and brooding. "No."

Edie nodded with a small smile, unsurprised by his answer.

Cliff turned around, unscrewing his bottle of antacid pills and popping two more in his mouth. He wasn't sure what was doing it, the chili dogs or her, but his stomach was on fire.

He pulled his logbook and a pencil out of his duffel bag and flipped it open. Noting the time on his wristwatch, he wrote it down, along with the words *Nothing to report*. Walt was a stickler for paperwork and he liked hourly written reports of everything that happened, even if nothing did.

Why did she have to light all the candles? The question jumped unbidden into his brain. They filled the room with a pleasing mixture of scents and created intimate pools of light that danced in her hair and softened the contours of her face, giving her skin a warm glow. Why didn't she just go to bed? Was she sitting up on purpose to unnerve him?

He had a clear view of her reflection in the window. She was sitting sideways, staring off into space pensively. He had a perfect view of the curve of her cheekbone, the straight line of her nose, the slightly defiant thrust of her chin. His gaze lingered on the length of her graceful neck, fully exposed by the braid that fell down her back. What would she look like with her hair loose and flowing? The tip of the pencil he'd been holding suddenly snapped against the page in the notebook.

"Damn." The single word exploded like a fire-cracker at dawn, shattering the quiet of the room.

"What's wrong?" She jumped, startled.

"I broke my pencil lead," Cliff answered, turning to look at her as if she was personally responsible.

Edie stared at him in amazement. "Do you always get so excited about life's little aggravations?"

"How the hell am I supposed to keep meticulous reports without a pencil?" He knew he was overre-acting. He also knew his reaction had nothing to do with the broken pencil lead.

Edie got up from the sofa and went to a kitchen drawer, where she took out a pencil, then walked over and offered it to him.

"Thanks," he murmured, flashing her a look of shame mingled with embarrassment.

The look was devastating to Edie, as devastating as if he'd intimately touched her. She'd come to expect anger and rudeness from him, but the momentary look he'd given her had been filled with a vulnerabil-ity that added a new, appealing dimension to the man. For a long moment their gazes remained locked. She was close enough to him that she could feel the heat from his body, see the rough texture of his whisker-darkened skin. She was vaguely conscious of her pulse beat quickening, and with a flush she broke the eye contact that had held her as effectively as a pin holds a butterfly to a display board.

"I—I think I'll go to bed. Blow out the candles, will you?" She didn't wait for an acknowledgment or an-swer from him. Instead, she fled the room. The last sound she heard was the rattle of his bottle of antacid tablets.

She punched the Snooze button on her alarm, lingering in the pleasant state between sound sleep and full consciousness. Edie had never been good at mornings. Nanny used to tease that nobody should talk to Edie in the mornings until she'd had a glass of juice and an hour to stare blankly into space. "That girl gives new meaning to the word cranky," Nanny would say with a laugh. Edie was well aware of her shortcomings concerning mornings. That was why she always arose early, so she could get all her crankiness out of her system before Nanny woke up.

When the alarm rang again, she jabbed at the offending instrument, silencing it with a quick right jab. She pulled herself out of bed, her body responding by habit but her brain not yet fully functioning.

Vision still blurry with sleep, she padded out of her bedroom and into the kitchen, needing a glass of orange juice to stimulate her still-sleeping head.

She opened the refrigerator door and grabbed the pitcher of juice, then poured herself a glass and brought it to her lips, at the same time turning around. With a screech of surprise she let the glass fall from her hand, and it shattered at her feet.

Three

―――

"Why didn't you say something?" She glared at him accusingly. "Why didn't you clear your throat or do something to remind me that you were here?"

Cliff said nothing, but his eyes spoke volumes. Dark and hot, they played over her body, igniting the heat of fire wherever they touched. Edie was suddenly conscious of the brevity of the teddy she was wearing. The peach-colored, lacy top was nearly transparent, exposing the rounded firmness of her breasts. Her nipples were rosy and taut, responding to the intensity of his gaze by pushing impudently against the thin material that confined them. She had never felt so totally feminine, never been so aware of herself, so conscious of her desirability as a woman, until this moment, with that desirability reflected in the dark orbs of his eyes. It both frightened her and excited her. She wasn't even aware that she had taken a step forward until she felt a sharp, throbbing pain pierce her foot. She gasped in surprise and lifted her foot, feeling weak-kneed as she saw the glitter of a shard of glass embedded in her heel and the rich redness of her blood oozing from the wound.

"Oh . . . I stepped on a piece of glass," she said in bewilderment, hobbling over to the couch where she sat down, placing the cut foot on a magazine on the coffee table.

Cliff was immediately out of his chair. "Do you have a first-aid kit?" His voice was deep with concern.

She nodded. "On the second shelf in the linen closet in the bathroom." She felt dazed, unsure whether her feeling of bewilderment came from the shock and pain of cutting her foot, or the confusing, almost frightening emotions she'd felt seconds before.

Cliff was back in a moment, carrying the first-aid kit. He sat on the coffee table facing her and placed her foot in his lap. "Does it hurt?"

"A little," she admitted. But she was having difficulty focusing on the pain. Instead, she felt the gentle pressure of his fingertips on her foot . . . and his warm concern washing over her, overriding the soreness in her heel.

"I'm afraid I'm going to hurt you." He looked up at her, his eyes unrevealing, giving her the impression that he was talking about much more than her foot.

"It's all right. I'm not breakable." Her voice was but a whisper, and she wondered if she, too, was talking about more than just the glass in her heel. For a long moment she simply stared at him, mesmerized by the strength of his features.

"I've got to pull out the glass." He broke their locked gaze, looking back down at her bleeding foot.

Edie closed her eyes and tensed, anticipating the pain. Instead, she was surprised by the infinite gentleness of his touch as he efficiently extracted the shining sliver.

"All done," he said, taking a bottle of antiseptic and several cotton balls from the first-aid kit.

"You don't have to do that," Edie murmured as he began to clean the wound.

"I can do it more easily than you can. Besides, I feel partially responsible. I startled you and made you drop the glass." His attention remained focused on his task.

As he cleaned her foot, Edie studied him, wondering what he would look like clean shaven. Beneath the dark shadows of his whiskers his features were well-defined—high cheekbones, the hint of a dimple at the left corner of his mouth, a firm chin. Her gaze lingered on his lips. He had a nice mouth when he wasn't holding it so grimly. At the moment, as he concentrated on his task, his mouth was relaxed, displaying a sensual fullness to his bottom lip that hadn't been evident before. His mouth looked strong, capable, and she wondered what it would feel like against her own.

Suddenly he was too close. She was too aware of him, the broadness of his shoulders, the strength of his thighs beneath her foot. She was overwhelmed by the soft, almost caressing quality of his touch as he finished cleaning the cut and covered it with a bandage. Still, his hands didn't leave her foot. Instead, as gently as butterfly wings against the fragile petals of a flower, his fingers moved up her foot, lightly touching her ankle, then caressing upward, lingering over the curve of her calf muscle.

A heavy languor stole over her, as if her blood had thickened, making each heartbeat a thunderous boom in her chest. He stroked the curve of her leg, as if enjoying the feel of her skin, and each stroke caused an exquisite ache of desire to surge through Edie's veins.

"Hello? Somebody come and get me out of this blasted bed." Nanny's strident voice came from the bedroom, shattering the moment, pulling Cliff and Edie back to reality, back from their momentary lapse into dangerous, unexplored territory.

Cliff's hand jerked away from her and as their eyes met she saw a flicker of surprise, like a sleepwalker who suddenly awakens to find himself in the middle of his front yard.

"It's time for me to pack it up." His voice was brusque as he jumped up and turned away from her. His movements were jerky and tense as he began shoving items back into the duffel bags.

Edie sat unmoving for a moment, still stunned by the knowledge that his touch had affected her so intensely. As his hand had caressed her leg she hadn't wanted him to stop. She'd wanted him to continue, his lips to follow the invisible map his hands had drawn.

She frowned suddenly, caught in a maelstrom of confusion. How could she want him physically when she hardly knew him, wasn't even sure she liked him?

She scoffed at her emotions. It had been a long time since she'd felt a man's touch on her. She probably would have responded to Attila the Hun if he had touched her leg.

"Help! Get me out of this bed." Nanny's plaintive request spurred Edie from her reverie. As she got up off the sofa, wincing slightly as she put weight on her bandaged foot, she saw that Cliff had packed up his equipment and was ready to leave. He got as far as the front door, then paused, his hand on the doorknob. He turned and looked at her. "You asked me last night if I was married and I said no." She nodded and he continued, his eyes cold and black as a wintry night. "I was married for three years."

"What happened?" She knew she had no right to ask, and there was no reason for him to tell her. But it suddenly seemed vital that she know. With his brooding eyes and irrational anger, he was like a perplexing jigsaw puzzle. Perhaps his answer would be a clue to solving the riddle of the man.

"She left me." His voice was flat and emotionless. Before she had a chance to ask anything more he was gone.

"You've got to take me off this case." Cliff sat across the desk from Walt. It was just after two o'clock in the afternoon and Cliff had yet to sleep since his all-night surveillance. Oh, it wasn't that he hadn't tried—he had. He'd tossed and turned and cursed the fates that had thrown him this job and Edie Turner.

"Impossible," Walt scoffed, then frowned. "You look like hell. I thought I told you to get a haircut."

"I look like hell because I haven't had any sleep for over twenty-four hours and I haven't had time to get a haircut." Cliff glowered. "Now, are you going to take me off this surveillance case or not?"

"Not," Walt replied firmly, then sighed. "Cliff, you know how shorthanded we always are in narcotics. I've gone out of my way to see to it that you have seen a lot of action in the last two years, but it's only fair that you take a turn at the drudgery aspect once in a while." Walt ran a hand through his thick white hair. "Is there a problem?"

"Not exactly. The grandmother thinks I'm some sort of voyeuristic pervert, and the granddaughter, Edith—" Cliff broke off, sighing heavily with frustration. What could he say? That Edith Turner was beautiful and that she had walked out of her bedroom in a skimpy peach-colored night thingy that had made his senses reel? He sighed in relief as a knock sounded on the office door.

"Enter," Walt commanded.

John Gibson, a fellow narcotics agent, walked into the office. "Hey, Marchelli," he greeted Cliff, then looked at Walt. "You wanted to see me, sir?"

"Sit down, I'll be with you in a minute." Walt gestured the young officer into a chair against the wall, then directed his attention to Cliff. "So, what's the problem with Edith Turner? Is she giving you a hard time?"

Cliff thought of her leg in his lap, the silky texture of her skin. "She's difficult," he finally blurted out desperately, his stomach rolling with suppressed emotion.

Walt's hand danced once again through his hair, making it stand straight up at attention. "Look, man, all I'm asking for is two weeks of your time. I know surveillance is easier when you don't have to do it in an occupied place, but in this particular situation, it's impossible. Edith's apartment is the best possible vantage point."

"Couldn't we move them out until we're finished?" Cliff asked in despair.

Walt shrugged. "I suppose we could, but that's a tightly knit area. People would talk, more people would hear. Moving Edith out would probably destroy the whole project. And there's also the matter of our limited budget. Paying for somebody to stay out of their house for two weeks would be quite expensive." Walt sighed. "Cliff, try to make this work." He looked at Cliff urgently. "There's a lot of activity generating from that warehouse. I want this bust. I retire in less than six months, and if this bust goes down right I'll go out of office in a blaze of glory."

Cliff wanted to protest. He wanted to run as far as possible from this particular assignment. But as he looked into the eyes of the man who had been not only boss but friend for the past thirteen years, he knew he'd see the assignment through to the end. It was the least he could do for the man who'd helped save his sanity the past two years.

"All right." Cliff relented, a hand unconsciously going to his stomach where his old, familiar friend of an ulcer was proclaiming its displeasure. He stood.

"I'll finish the surveillance, but you owe me for this one."

Walt relaxed, visibly relieved at Cliff's capitulation. "Right, and I'll pay you back as soon as you see a doctor about that ulcer."

"Yeah, right." Cliff grinned wryly, knowing he would do no such thing. He nodded at John and Walt, then left the office.

He knew he should go home and get a couple of hours' sleep before going back to the Turner apartment that evening, but at the moment sleep was the farthest thing from his mind.

Instead, he found himself driving aimlessly, his mind filled with tormenting visions of Edie Turner. He'd known the instant she had walked into the living room that morning that she was still asleep enough to have forgotten his presence. He'd known that he should cough, or clear his throat, or do something to signal to her that he was there. But from the moment she'd stumbled into the room he'd been incapable of speech, utterly powerless to move. He'd found himself sinking into forgotten emotions, remembering long-denied feelings.

It had been a very long time since he had felt desire, remembered the exquisite pleasure that came with making love. He'd buried that emotion when his wife had walked out on him. He didn't want to feel desire. He didn't want to feel anything. But Edie had made him feel the first stirrings of life he'd felt for over two years. And it scared the hell out of him.

* * *

For a long moment after Cliff had left, Edie stood staring at the door, her mind contemplating his final words.

"She left me." Never had she heard words uttered so devoid of emotion, so barren of life. As she swept up the last of the shattered glass, his words continued to plague her. What had happened to the marriage? What had gone wrong? The questions were shoved to the back of her mind as she got Nanny out of bed and concentrated on fixing breakfast.

After eating, Edie led Nanny to the sofa and turned on the television, then placed a shoe box of costume jewelry on her lap. Nanny smiled like a child given a treasured box of blocks, her hands moving reverently over the colorful paste creations.

With Nanny quietly occupied, Edie began to clean up the breakfast dishes. *I wonder what his wife was like,* she thought as she scraped off the plates and put them into the dishwasher. *Probably a saint if she put up with him. What kind of a husband was he?* she wondered as she wiped down the surface of the stove. How could she even begin to guess the answer? She knew nothing about him. *Well, almost nothing,* she qualified, remembering the singeing intensity of his dark eyes as they had ravished her. *Ravish* . . . such a strong word, conjuring up images of innocent virgins and bold heroes. Well, she wasn't an innocent and he certainly wasn't a hero. Yet, as his umbrageous eyes had lingered on her scantily clad physique, she'd felt the shuddery anticipation of a newly wedded bride going to her marriage bed.

"Edie, dear, are you awake?" Rose's voice and loud knock at the door startled Edie, who realized she'd been staring blankly at the gleaming stove top, sponge poised in midair. She threw the sponge into the sink, then went to admit Rose.

"Good morning, Rose." Edie smiled at her neighbor.

"It's not a good morning," Rose said, going to the table and planting her solid bottom firmly in a chair. "Do you have a cup of tea for a poor, miserable soul?" She looked at Edie mournfully.

Edie nodded, putting the teakettle on the stove and wondering what had caused Rose's flair for melodrama to rise to the surface. "So, tell me, Rose, what has you so upset that you need a cup of my herbal tea?" Edie asked, joining Rose at the table.

"Anthony and his prospective bride."

"But I thought you were happy that Anthony is getting married," Edie protested.

"I was . . . I am, but this Sherri person that my Anthony has chosen to marry, she doesn't want any children." Rose's broad face screwed up in abject misery. "Now the name of Tonnilesco will die and I'll never have grandchildren." Fat teardrops chased each other down her cheeks.

Steam spewing from the teakettle delayed Edie's answer. She poured them each a cup of the decaffeinated herbal tea, checked that Nanny was still happily preoccupied with her jewelry, then sat down at the table.

"She's a schoolteacher, and she says she gets enough kids all day long." The tears on Rose's face dried as quickly as water drops on a hot griddle, and instead rightful indignation sparked in her dark eyes. "What kind of a woman doesn't want children?"

Edie smiled, realizing that to one of Rose's generation the idea of choosing not to have children was completely foreign. "Rose, a lot of people these days are making the decision not to have children."

"What kind of a decision is that?" Vexation crinkled her face. "You'd want children, wouldn't you?"

Edie thought a long moment before answering. Yes, at one time she had longed to have a baby. Unfortunately there had been no man with whom she'd wanted to share her life. That particular dilemma had yet to be altered. She had shoved her maternal longings out of her mind. Besides, taking care of Nanny fulfilled much of Edie's nurturing need. "I really don't know," she finally answered, then grinned. "I seem to be missing some very important ingredients in my life if I want to have children."

"Well, whose fault is that?" Rose demanded. "I've told you and told you that I'll watch your grandmother any night so you can go out and socialize. And the rare nights you do go out, you date that Dr. Prissy-Pants Powers." Rose's face reflected her dislike of Marcus Powers. "And how can he love anyone? He's too busy loving himself."

Edie laughed. Prissy-pants . . . yes, she had to admit Marcus was something of a narcissist. "Marcus is okay," she said with a grin. "As long as I don't take him too seriously."

"But that's exactly my point, Edie, darling." Rose paused long enough to sip her tea, then continued.

"It's time you found a man for yourself, somebody who you *can* take seriously. Taking care of your grandmother is fine, but you're a healthy young woman and you need more in your life than a little old woman." Edie opened her mouth to protest, but her efforts were as effective as those of a flower against a marauding bulldozer. "You know, Edie, you aren't getting any younger. Your biological clock is ticking away."

"I'm only thirty years old," Edie said with a laugh.

Rose shrugged her shoulders. "One day you're thirty...then thirty-five...then forty...and before you know it, poof, you're too old to have a family."

"I have a family." Edie looked over at Nanny fondly.

Rose reached across the table and patted Edie's hand. "And what you're doing, taking care of Nanny, it's a good thing to do. Too many people are in too big a hurry to put us old people away in nursing homes. But darling, don't sacrifice your own life for your grandmother's sake. Life is too short and love is too hard to find."

"Don't worry, Rose." Edie squeezed Rose's hand affectionately. "Someday I'll find my Prince Charming and we'll get married, have a houseful of kids and live happily ever after. I'll tell you what, I'll even name you as godmother to all my children."

Rose swallowed the last of her tea and stood. "One thing is for certain. Your Prince Charming isn't going to just waltz right in that door."

Edie immediately thought of Cliff Marchelli. He had waltzed right through her door, but he certainly didn't qualify as Prince Charming material. Still, it was an interesting thought, the fairy-tale concept that a kiss could turn a toad into a prince.

Cliff watched as a large delivery truck crept slowly down the street toward the warehouse. Adrenaline began pumping through his veins as the large paneled truck pulled in to the warehouse driveway. Maybe this was it—the night of the big buy. Then he could get out of this apartment and away from Edie Turner, away from the indefinable tension that lingered in the air between them. The adrenaline escaped through a disappointed sigh as the delivery truck turned around in the driveway and drove off in the direction from which it had come.

From the moment he had entered the apartment a half hour before, he and Edie had studiously ignored each other. But just because he wasn't looking at her didn't mean he wasn't aware of her. How could he not be when her fragrance filled the room and surrounded his senses? How could he not be conscious of her as she bustled around in the kitchen, hurrying to get their evening meal on the table before darkness stole in, sucking the sunlight out of the room like a monster whose main diet was light. The sound of dishes clattering, the melodic noise of her humming as she worked made him remember evenings from long ago when he would sit in his kitchen, watching Catherine preparing their evening meal.

Funny, thoughts of Catherine had always brought with them an incredible anger, a rage so intense it twisted his guts inside out. This time the anger was much less intense, mingling with a new sadness.

"Cliff, would you like to have some lasagna with us?"

He turned away from the window and looked at Edie, surprised by the invitation to share their meal. He quickly assessed his alternatives—the lasagna that filled the room with its rich aroma, or the two cheeseburgers shoved into his duffel bag, probably congealed with grease and unrecognizable in shape.

"Yeah, okay," he agreed. "If it's not any trouble."

"No trouble. I'll just set another plate on the table," she answered.

"No." The word was sharp with alarm. "I...I...uh, can't leave my post here at the window. If it's all right, I'll just take a plate right here." He turned back around, a light flush covering his face, knowing her eyes lingered on him curiously. He'd completely overreacted, but he didn't want to join them at the table. It would seem too normal, too much like a real family. And family, happiness, happily ever after were all concepts Cliff never allowed himself to fantasize about, not anymore.

"Sure, no problem," Edie agreed, her eyes searching his broad back as if she could discover the quintessence of the inner man.

From the moment he'd walked in she'd felt an unaccustomed shyness, coupled with the desire to know him better. She'd extended the invitation for him to eat with them in hopes that sitting at their table, sharing their food would stimulate some form of sociability from him. She wasn't fool enough to expect instant gregariousness, but she'd hoped to get him to at least grunt more than one-syllable answers and not glare like a bear whose winter sleep had been disturbed.

"I'll wake up Nanny and we'll eat in just a few minutes." She waited until she saw his almost imperceptible nod, then she went into the bedroom to awaken Nanny from her nap.

"Nanny, wake up. It's time for supper." Edie gently shook the older woman's shoulder. Nanny's eyes opened, and as Edie looked into their blue warmth she realized she was seeing the woman who'd raised her, the woman she loved. Edie cherished the sight, which was happening less and less frequently.

"Ah, Edie." Nanny reached up and touched Edie's face lovingly, her wrinkled hand lingering on Edie's cheek. "I was having the most wonderful dream. We were all at a lovely tea party, and my mama was there and your mama was there, and we were drinking our tea out of beautiful china cups and eating little pastries."

"That sounds wonderful, Nanny." Edie helped her to a sitting position. "Now it's time to get up and eat dinner."

Nanny patted Edie's face gently. "You're such a good girl, Edie. You've always been the light of my life." Before Edie could answer, the light of recognition faded from her grandmother's eyes.

"And you're mine," Edie whispered, silently saying goodbye to the woman she loved. By the time she had her grandmother out of bed Nanny had regressed to a spunky stranger who waved away Edie's efforts to escort her from the bedroom.

"What's he doing here?" Nanny asked, pointing a finger in Cliff's direction as she sat down at the table. "Doesn't he have a home to go to?"

"Cliff has come to visit," Edie said, taking the large baking dish of lasagna from the oven.

"Pretty damn rude, isn't he," Nanny replied. "He comes over to visit, then sits staring out the window." Nanny scowled. "I thought Bessie had more sense than to raise such an unmannerly boy."

Edie opened her mouth to protest Nanny's assessment of Cliff's character, then snapped her mouth closed. Why should she defend him?

"I'm sorry, I didn't mean to be rude." Edie was surprised to hear him defend himself. She was further surprised to see him turn sideways in his chair and offer a tentative smile at Nanny.

The smile, so unexpected, so achingly vulnerable, caused Edie's breath to catch in her throat. Nanny nodded, mollified by his answer. "Now, if you'd scrape some of that hair off your face you'd look almost civilized."

Cliff nodded, his upper lip twitching in what appeared to be amusement.

Edie turned away, busying herself with slicing up the loaf of Italian bread. His little half smile had illuminated his features with life, and the small curve of his lips had promised what he would look like if he ever relaxed enough to smile not only with his lips but with his heart, as well. Somehow, deep within, she knew she wouldn't be satisfied until she experienced a full, heartfelt smile from him.

She turned to see Nanny still studying Cliff. "You know, you don't look a bit like Bessie," Nanny mused. "I guess you favor your father. He was a real looker. Had that dark hair and dark eyes, sort of like Clark Gable, but oh, what a scoundrel he was."

Cliff looked at Edie helplessly, obviously unsure how to answer.

"Yes, Cliff looks just like his father," Edie replied, setting both the bread and a tossed salad on the table. She added the lasagna and began fixing Cliff a plate.

"I thought we were having tacos," Nanny exclaimed. "Wouldn't you rather have tacos than this stuff?" she asked Cliff.

"Lasagna's good," Cliff answered. In fact, his mouth watered at the thought of rich, cheesy lasagna with thick, spiced meat sauce. It had been a long time since he'd eaten anything other than things high in cholesterol and low in nutrition that came wrapped in cellophane or in a foam disposable box.

"Hrrumph, lasagna's good, but tacos are better," Nanny announced.

"Thanks," Cliff murmured as Edie handed him the filled plate. As she rejoined her grandmother at the table, he looked at the lasagna with a frown. Granted, it had been a while since he'd eaten the Italian dish, but the layered block of noodles on his plate didn't begin to resemble what he knew as lasagna. Where was the sauce? Where was the meat? He took his fork and cut into it, his frown deepening as he saw chunks of indefinable green stuff.

"Is something wrong?" Edie asked.

"No...it's just...where's the meat?" he finally managed to sputter in bewilderment.

"Oh, there is no meat. Nanny and I are vegetarians."

"She's a vegetarian, I'm just a prisoner at her mercy," Nanny quipped.

"I always make vegetable lasagna. It's so much better for you than all that red meat and heavy spices."

"I like red meat and heavy spices," Cliff muttered, realizing the green chunks were pieces of broccoli and spinach.

"Yes, but it's obvious your stomach doesn't like red meat and spices. How long have you had your ulcer?"

"I don't have an ulcer," he grumbled, resenting her intrusion into his personal business.

"I guess you just chew those antacid tablets because you like the taste of chalk," Edie returned with a small grin. "I suppose as a child you were one of the boys who always ate the chalk at the blackboard."

The image her words presented made amusement suddenly bubble out of him. Like Old Faithful spewing water into the air at a totally unexpected time, his laughter surprised him. And then, because he'd forgotten how good it felt to laugh, he did it again.

The sound of his rich laughter reached inside and plucked persistently at Edie's heartstrings, and her heart responded by pelting against her chest.

His laughter slowly died and for a long moment their gazes remained locked.

"Are you two going to sit there and stare at each other all night, or are we gonna eat?" Nanny asked in exasperation.

Before Edie's very eyes he transformed, changing back into the somber, brooding man whose dark eyes offered only the coldness of wintry air. "We're going to eat," he replied, turning around in his chair and presenting his back to them.

Frustration clung to Edie like a tenacious tick, making her hands shake slightly as she filled plates for Nanny and herself. Damn, for a moment he had almost acted human. He seemed to guard himself so closely, afraid to share any part of himself. His laughter had escaped in an incautious moment, when his defensive sentinel had been relaxed.

As she ate she wondered how many other qualities besides his laughter he kept firmly tucked and hidden away. She also wondered what it would take to make a crack in that hardened facade, a crack big enough for her to crawl through.

It wasn't until after dinner that Edie once again saw a sign of vulnerability in him. Nanny was back in bed and Edie and Cliff were alone except for the advancing shadows of darkness filling the room.

"I feel a little like Abraham Lincoln," she said as she lit a candle next to her word processor on the table.

"Yes, but I don't think he had the luxury of a word processor and a dictating machine," Cliff answered. "Still, I know it's inconvenient to have to work in the dark. What exactly is it you type?"

"I'm a medical transcriber and word processor. I was working in an office of six doctors but a couple of months ago I quit the office to be here and take care of Nanny. The doctors were kind enough to allow me to do the work at home. Normally I don't work this late, but I have some reports that need to be finished by tomorrow and I didn't have a chance to get to them today." Emboldened by the fact that he was being civil, she ventured a question. "How long have you been on the police force?"

"It will be fourteen years in June. I became a cop when I was twenty-one."

"Do you like the work?"

It took him so long to answer Edie began to wonder if he'd forgotten the question. Just as she was about to repeat it, he spoke. "Yes, I like my work." He turned and looked at her. "In the last couple of years my work has been the most important thing in my life. What about you? Do you like what you do?"

She nodded. "Sure, it's interesting and right now it's the best thing I could be doing. This transcribing work allows me the freedom to be here with Nanny and still pay the bills. She needs me."

"You're good at it, taking care of her. You obviously have lots of patience."

"It's easy to be patient with somebody you love," she replied softly. Their eyes met and held for a long moment. Electricity charged the air. She'd seen his eyes darkened with suppressed anger. She'd seen them cold with studied indifference. But this time, as they lingered on her, they were lit with a silken, passionate light that held her motionless. Like a ballerina on the top of a box held captive by the music that made her dance, Edie was lost, a prisoner to the fires that smoldered in his eyes.

They both jumped as a knock sounded on the door.

"Don't let anyone in," Cliff cautioned. The look that had held her captive was gone, as if it had never existed, making her wonder if she had only imagined the longing in his eyes.

She nodded and went to the door, opening it only a couple of inches.

"Pizza delivery." On the other side of the door a dark-haired young man in a red-and-white-striped delivery shirt stood holding a pizza box.

"You must have made a mistake. We didn't order any pizza." Edie started to close the door, but the man stuck his foot between it and the jamb.

"This is a delivery for Cliff Marchelli," he said pointedly, flashing her a badge hidden beneath the collar of the uniform.

"Cliff, it's for you." She opened the door to admit the man.

"Hey, Marchelli." He grinned at Cliff.

"Gibson, what are you doing here?" Cliff stood and greeted him, then turned to Edie. "This is John Gibson. We work together."

Edie nodded, then sat back down at the table and placed her Dictaphone earphones over her ears. Not wanting to intrude on their work, she began to move her fingers nimbly over the keys. Still, she couldn't help but overhear the conversation going on between the two men.

"How do you like my cover?" John grinned at Cliff and smoothed the red-and-white-striped shirt he was wearing.

"Terrific. So what are you doing here?"

"The captain sent me with these." He opened the pizza box and withdrew what appeared to Edie to be several photographs. "Word out is that one of these men will be our buyer."

"Thanks." Cliff studied the photographs.

"Can she hear us?" John asked, his voice just audible over the clicking of her keyboard.

Cliff shook his head absently.

"So that's the infamous Edith Turner," John said in amusement.

Edie stiffened, her fingers not pausing as she continued typing.

"I can't believe you were in the captain's office today griping about how difficult she is. She doesn't look so bad to me. In fact, she looks pretty good."

"Yeah, right." Cliff led him to the door. "Thanks for bringing the photos and tell the captain I'll check in with him in the morning." With this, Cliff shoved John out the door and shot an uneasy smile at Edie.

Edie jerked up out of her chair and faced him, anger making her eyes flash as she tore off her earphones. "You are despicable. I can't believe you went to Mr. Cummings and said I was difficult. I volunteered my apartment, hoping to help the police in some way, but you come in here with a chip on your shoulder the size of a boulder, then have the audacity to complain about me." She stalked over to him, standing mere inches from where he stood. "Let me tell you something, Cliff Marchelli. You are a toad, and I have a feeling if I would kiss you, you'd still be a toad.'' With these words she stormed out of the room and into her bedroom, the slamming of her door punctuating her final sentence.

Four

Cliff stared at the closed bedroom door, remorse
mingling with confusion. He was sorry she'd over-
heard John and he now regretted the impulse that had
sent him running to Walt's office. But what in the hell
had she meant with all that talk about toads?

He sat in his chair at the window and picked up his
bottle of antacid pills. As he started to shake two out
into his palm, he changed his mind and screwed the lid
back on the bottle. He'd reached for them out of
habit, because of the turmoil with Edie, but his stomach didn't need them. In fact, his stomach felt better
than it had in months and he had to admit it was
probably due to his ingesting the mild, nutritious vegetable lasagna instead of his usual fare of spicy, greasy
fast foods.

He got up and walked over to the table where she had been working, noticing the luminous digital display readout. She had been so angry she hadn't even bothered to shut off the machine before stomping off. He located the right button and switched it off, then blew out the candles and returned to his chair at the window.

A smile moved the corners of his lips upward as he thought of the woman in the other room. She certainly had no problems displaying her emotions. She didn't swallow her anger and let it fester in her stomach. She let it all hang out. She would never get ulcers. His smile widened. She was the type who would give others ulcers.

Still, he had to admit, with her standing so close to him, her chest heaving with emotion, her eyes snapping with ire, he was tempted. Tempted to do what? He'd wanted to pull her up against him, feel how their bodies fit together in an intimate embrace. He'd felt the need to press his lips against hers, hold her until the fire of anger in her eyes was replaced with the fire of desire.

He gave a small snort of self-derision and ran a hand over his whisker-roughened chin. Yeah, right, he was sure she was just dying to kiss him. Every woman at one time or another in their life had a strong desire to kiss a scouring pad.

A shave wouldn't hurt, he thought, staring up at the three-quarter moon in the dark sky. His hand moved from his chin to the back of his neck, his fingers tugging unconsciously at the hair that fell over his shirt collar. A haircut wouldn't hurt, either. He jerked his hand away from his hair. He was fine just the way he was. He wasn't about to make changes in his appearance for anyone.

He looked up once again at the chunk of moon and thought about the woman on the other side of the closed bedroom door. Since seeing her that morning in her peach-colored sleeping thing, he had found it easy to visualize the way she would look lying in bed. Her dark hair would be loose, like spilled coffee staining the whiteness of a linen tablecloth. No fetal curl for Edie, oh, no. Somebody as open and giving as she would sleep flat on her back, leaving herself exposed and vulnerable to nighttime caressing and languid lovemaking.

A slow heat began building in him as the mental images intensified. Like a psychedelic light show, illusions flashed across his brain, stunning him with their seductive quality...Edie, her arms open and beckoning him to join her on the bed. Edie, standing in the moonlight, shrugging out of the nightie to expose her moon-kissed curves, her eyes an open invitation to him.

The heat suddenly centered in the core of his stomach. Sweat beaded on his brow and he fought internally against the dangerous emotions that railed in him.

He wanted her. The acceptance of that fact somehow eased his battle. Why shouldn't he want her? She was a beautiful, desirable woman and he was a healthy man with a sexual appetite he'd suppressed for too long. It was only natural that he should feel physical desire. It was okay to feel that need as long as he didn't follow through on it. The real sin would be if he made love to her and gave her the mistaken impression that he could give her more than physical fulfillment. Cliff knew he couldn't offer more. Where his heart had once been was now just an abyss—black...dead... empty.

"Cliff?"

He jumped and swore, turning to see her standing in the doorway.

"I'm sorry, I didn't mean to startle you." She moved closer to him, belting her terry-cloth robe more securely around her slender waist. "I want to ask you something."

"What?" He refused to look at her. The erotic fantasies of moments before were still too fresh in his mind for him to be comfortable looking at her.

"Why do you think I'm difficult?"

Cliff sighed heavily and ran a hand through his hair in distraction. "Just forget about it. It's not important."

"But it is important," she pressed, moving another step toward him.

"I really don't want to have this conversation." What he wanted to do was run far away, leave her and this apartment behind.

"But I do." Edie frowned as she saw him reach for his bottle of pills. "Is your stomach bothering you?" She didn't wait for an answer. Instead she went to the refrigerator and poured him a large glass of milk. "Here, drink this instead of taking those pills. You must spend a fortune on them."

He took the glass from her and drained it, then handed it back. Edie set the glass on the table, then returned to her spot close to him. "Now, tell me why you think I'm so difficult."

Cliff winced and rubbed his stomach. "What are you trying to do? Sour the milk you just gave me?" he grumbled. "Just let it go, drop it." He turned his back to her.

"You know, you wouldn't have such stomach problems if you didn't hold everything inside." Edie stared at his broad back for a long moment. "It's obvious from what your friend said earlier that you went to Walt and complained about me. I think it's only fair you tell me why."

She gasped as he whirled around and out of the chair and grabbed her wrists, pulling her tightly against the hard length of his body. In the moonlight spilling through the window she could see his eyes, a dark intensity of suppressed emotion, his face hardened with anger and something else . . . something she couldn't quite define.

"You don't think I should hold my emotions inside? Fine, then I'll tell you exactly why I find you difficult." His voice was a rasp, his breath hot and heavy against her face, making her shiver involuntarily. "You're difficult because your skin is so soft, and your hair . . . I could get lost in it." One hand left her wrist to tangle in her hair. "And your lips, they're just begging to be kissed."

Edie's breath escaped her body in a slow hiss. She was vaguely conscious that he no longer held her wrists, that she was free to move away from him, free to escape. But escape was the farthest thing from her mind. His words had spun a seductive web around her, tangling her up, holding her rooted to the spot. She knew she should run, but she couldn't. She knew he was going to kiss her and she wanted it.

His mouth took hers in an explosive demand, and the last vestige of thought deserted her. She opened her lips to him, her body arching against his, instinctively seeking the perfect fit against the hard angles and planes his body offered.

He moaned and deepened the kiss, pressing harder, his tongue touching first the edge of her teeth, then thrusting into every corner of her mouth. His hands tangled themselves in her hair, dragging her head back to expose the curve of her throat.

Edie was lost in sensation, drunk on the taste of him, the feel of him, disoriented by her urgent, primitive response to him.

"I've wanted this from the moment I first walked into this apartment," he murmured as he pulled his mouth from hers. She hardly heard him, dizzy from the power of his violent kiss. Her blood pounded in her veins, her breath coming from her in uneven gasps.

He tilted his torso back and looked at her, his eyes all darkness and heat. "You don't want me to hold everything inside, then I'll tell you why I find you difficult. I want you, Edie."

The starkness of the words made her breath catch painfully in her throat. He pressed his hips harder against hers, making her completely aware of the intensity of his arousal. "I want to take you into the bedroom and place you on the bed. Then I want to replace your clothes with my lips." His eyes darkened, flashing with the look of the haunted. "But don't get confused. What I want to share with you has nothing to do with love. You'd be just a pleasant interlude in my life, brief and passionate, but a momentary thing, at best." His eyes softened slightly. "And something tells me you aren't the kind of woman to settle for that." He took a deep breath and continued. "So, now you know what I want from you and why I think you're being so difficult." He released her suddenly, dropping his hands to his sides with a weary sigh. "Go to bed, Edie. If we're both very lucky, in a week or so I'll be out of here and out of your life." He turned and sat back down, his silhouette in the window looking somehow vulnerable... and very lonely.

He wanted her. As Edie ran for the safety of her bedroom, she found the knowledge both exhilarating and frightening. She sat on the edge of the bed, touching softly the lips he had devoured moments before. He'd made her feel things she didn't want to feel. He'd made her remember she had been neglecting her own needs in her efforts to care for her grandmother. He was Casanova, seducing her with his practiced technique, the devil tempting her soul. And temptation was so wonderfully delicious, so entrancingly inviting.

She took off her robe, then crawled beneath the sheets and shut off the bedside lamp. He'd been trying to scare her, to warn her away from him, but she was drawn to him like a child to matches, irresistibly drawn to the fire even though the result is usually a burn.

He was a hard case, but she had a feeling that the woman who managed to crack his shell would be the luckiest woman in the world. It would take a lot of patience, but as she'd told him earlier, she could be very patient with those people she cared about.

She sat straight up in the bed, shock tingling her nerve endings as a sudden thought niggled in the back of her brain. Was it possible she was beginning to care for Cliff? If so, she hoped the result wasn't ulcers for two.

The sun just peeked over the horizon, sending out streaks of light as forerunners testing the welcome. Cliff stretched tiredly, pulling down his shirt as it rode up the firm, flat plane of his stomach.

The sun was a welcome sight, banishing the darkness that had enshrouded the world. He just hoped it could banish the darkness of the emotions he'd wrestled with the past two nights.

Edie...her name made him hungry. The kiss he had stolen from her two nights earlier had been like a luscious appetizer that precedes a feast. It had merely served to make him hungry for the main course.

And in the time since that kiss she had skittered around him warily, going to her room soon after he arrived in the evenings and not coming out again until he was gone in the mornings. It had made things easier on him. But nothing could ease his conscience when he remembered their kiss.

He'd been brutal and raw with her, much more brutal than he'd intended. But he'd needed to shake her up, scare her away. From the moment they had met, the sexual tension had surged like an electric current in the air between them. He'd felt it and he knew she did, as well. He'd experienced the lick of passion before in the past two years. It was an old enemy that he'd learned to battle with hard physical exercise and steadfast, rigid control. But in that brief moment two nights ago, when he'd held her warm, curvaceous body in his arms, he'd felt his control slipping. It had taken every ounce of his willpower to push her away.

The past two nights had been endlessly long. He wondered what would have happened had he not distanced himself from her. She had certainly not fought against him. Rather she had accepted the kiss willingly, making his mind race with tormenting visions of *what if*s. He wouldn't have been surprised if the morning had found him dead, overdosed on antacid tablets with only erotic fantasies filling his logbook.

"Good morning."

He jumped at the sound of her sleep-huskied voice, surprised that she had decided to venture out of her bedroom before he left. He watched her move across the floor like a somnambulist with a penchant for raiding the refrigerator. She hadn't made the same mistake—there was no hint of the peach nightie, and every inch of her skin was covered by the voluminous caftan she wore.

"Morning," he murmured, his eyes lingering on her as she grabbed the pitcher of juice and tilted it to her mouth. A grin of amusement touched his lips.

Edie caught sight of his small smile. "And just what is so amusing?" she asked, cranky from two nights spent tossing and turning. She felt as if she hadn't slept in weeks and it was all his fault.

"My mother always spanked me for drinking straight from the pitcher." His smile wavered, mingling with a touch of bittersweetness as he remembered the many fights he'd had with his mother over his habit of drinking out of the milk jug. A wave of guilt swept over him as he realized how long it had been since he'd called and talked to his mother.

Edie saw the softening of his features, and her early-morning crossness dissipated somewhat. "Are you close to your mother?" She replaced the pitcher in the refrigerator.

"I used to be." His gaze grew distant. "She remarried and moved to St. Louis several years ago and since then we've sort of lost touch." He tried to remember how it had happened that he and his mother had grown distant. When had it been that he'd stopped calling her, and when had she finally given up and stopped calling him?

"That's too bad. I feel that life is too short to allow distance, whether physical or emotional, to separate us from those we love."

"Life is too short to bother getting emotionally involved with anyone."

She looked at him, surprised by the bitterness in his voice. "Oh, Cliff, you're so wrong. I'd rather have a fleeting moment of love than a full lifetime without it."

He looked at her for a long time, then grinned humorlessly. "Then you, Edith Turner, are a fool."

The ringing of the telephone preempted her reply. "Who could that be at this time of the morning?" she mumbled, hurrying to answer. "Hello? Hi, what's wrong? Tonight? Oh, I couldn't . . . I'm afraid it's impossible. I don't think I could get anyone to sit with Nanny." She paused a moment, then continued. "I suppose I could check and see if Rose would be available. I'll call you back and let you know."

"Is there a problem?" Cliff asked when she'd hung up.

"Friends of mine have tickets to the ballet tonight. They wanted me to go, too."

"You like the ballet?" he asked as he began loading up his equipment.

"I adore it," she exclaimed. "I think in another life I must have been a famous ballerina. Unfortunately, in this life I was gifted with no coordination and very little rhythm." She laughed suddenly, the sound full of a youthful abandonment that made him wish he could take her to the ballet every night, anything to make her laugh like that more often. Yet a part of him cringed at the very idea of attending a ballet. He wouldn't know a faux pas from a *bonjour,* or whatever those French ballet terms were.

"It's been so long since I've seen a ballet, and the performance tonight is one of my favorites, *Giselle.* " The words bubbled out of her as she fixed herself a cup of tea. She held out a cup to him, but he shook his head. She didn't eat meat, so he had a feeling her tea would be made of something like grass seed and betel-nut juice.

"And I suppose you took ballet lessons when you were young." He was packed up and ready to go, yet he found himself reluctant to leave. There was something rather intimate about sharing a conversation while dawn slowly crept in to fill the room with light and most of the rest of the people in the city still lay sleeping in their beds.

"Of course, doesn't every little girl at one time or another in her childhood take ballet lessons?" She smiled, sitting at the table with her cup of tea. "Once a week for two years I attended Madame Luxinski's Ballet Academy and dreamed of being a prima ballerina."

Cliff tried to imagine her as a young girl in a fluffy tutu, but every time he tried, all he could visualize were her long, shapely legs—definitely not the limbs of a child. "Why did you give it up?"

"On day at dance school I came out of my fantasies long enough to watch myself in the mirror. My first thought was, 'What is that poor, untalented girl doing?' Then I realized that poor, untalented girl was me, so I quit. I stopped dancing, but my love for the ballet has never diminished." She looked at him curiously. "What about you? What did you dream of being when you were young?"

"An astronomer." The confession surprised him. He hadn't thought of those boyhood yearnings for years. He smiled inwardly, shaking his head at the memories her question evoked. "I was given a telescope for Christmas when I was about eight years old and it opened up a whole new world for me. I spent hours studying stars, pretending I was a famous astronomer discovering new galaxies.''

''What happened to those dreams?'' Edie asked softly, realizing by the look on his face that he'd lost himself for a moment in the memories of innocent youth.

He smiled, a cynical twist of his lips. ''The last thing the world needed was another romantic stargazer.''

''Oh, I don't think everyone would ever accuse you of being that,'' Edie said with a grin.

''What? A stargazer?''

''No, a romantic.'' She giggled as he scowled.

''I've got to go,'' he said stiffly, walking to the front door. ''I'll see you tonight.'' He opened the door and stepped out into the hallway. He couldn't believe he'd told her about his childhood dreams of being an astronomer. That was something he'd never shared with Catherine. He felt that by telling Edie, he'd compromised himself, exposed a fragment he'd always jealously guarded. What was it about Edie Turner that inspired such confidences?

He jumped as the apartment door across the hall swung open and two dark eyes surveyed him suspiciously. ''It's awfully early in the morning for visitors.'' The door swung open to reveal a plump, older Italian woman dressed in a bathrobe, her hair in strange-looking pink curlers.

''I . . . uh . . . I was just leaving,'' he stuttered, tightening his grip on his duffel bags.

"Oh." Her eyes surveyed him once again, then looked at Edie's closed door. "Oh," she repeated, her eyes beginning to glow with a light that immediately made Cliff want to protest. "So, you're a friend of Edie's?" Her smile reminded him of an aunt he'd had who always managed to raise welts on his cheeks by pinching them affectionately. He took a step backward and stifled the impulse to raise his hands to his cheeks in self-defense.

"Yeah, a friend," Cliff said vaguely. Damn, the last thing he needed was a neighbor becoming suspicious as to why he was coming out of Edie's apartment so early in the morning. And something told him this particular neighbor would not exactly be the soul of discretion.

"My name is Rose Tonnilesco," she said, coming toward him, her hand extended in greeting. "And you're...?" Her dark eyebrows shot up, as if forming question marks to punctuate her inquiry.

"Uh...Cliff. Cliff Marchelli." He shook her hand, wondering desperately how to escape without compromising his assignment. He couldn't very well tell her what he was doing in the Turner apartment.

"Ah, a nice Italian man." Rose beamed her obvious approval. "I hope we'll be seeing more of you around here." She smiled coyly. "Edie's such a wonderful person."

"Yeah, she is," he agreed, suddenly realizing the way to cover his presence in the apartment. Rose apparently imagined a lover's tryst, so why disillusion her? "I'm sure you'll be seeing a lot more of me around here." He winked broadly, then giving her a jaunty wave he turned and headed for the stairs.

Edie had just finished her second cup of tea when Rose knocked on her door and walked in. "Ah, aren't you a sly one." Rose shook her finger at Edie, a grin decorating her broad face.

"What are you talking about?" Edie asked curiously.

"Here I've been worried about your social life and this morning I open my door to get the morning paper and what do I see? A man sneaking out of your apartment, and a nice Italian man, at that."

Edie laughed in sudden comprehension. "That wasn't a man, that was Cliff. I mean, he's a man, but..." Her voice trailed off as she realized her dilemma. It was obvious Rose thought he had spent the night with her in the romantic sense. Now, how could she explain to the older woman that she was wrong without jeopardizing Cliff's professional position? She of all people knew Rose's love for gossip. It was a standing joke in the apartment that if somebody wanted to speak to all the tenants, they had only to tell Rose. "Rose, you have it all wrong. Cliff is...uh...just a friend."

"I should be so lucky to have a friend like that," Rose replied, a wicked little gleam in her dark eyes. "He's got cute buns." She laughed at Edie's expression of shock. "What's the matter, I surprise you? You think that because I'm old and widowed, I don't notice things like that? He definitely looked like a hunk to me."

"Yes, but I'm still trying to figure out—a hunk of what?" Edie replied dryly.

"So, tell me about him," Rose demanded. "I want to know everything."

"There's really nothing to tell," Edie said helplessly, knowing that no matter what she said Rose was going to believe what she wanted. "Honestly, we're just friends. As a matter of fact, I was going to come over to see you this morning to ask you a favor. Would you be available to watch Nanny this evening?"

"Sure, she can spend the night at my place." Rose winked slyly. "You maybe have special plans with this Cliff?"

Edie shook her head. "Some friends have tickets to the ballet."

"I'll be glad to have Nanny over. Just bring her over as you go out." Rose's grin widened. "And I'll get out of here now so you can relax before the ballet. I'm sure you could use some rest after last night." She shook her finger at Edie. "And sooner or later you're going to have to tell me all about this Cliff." With an uncharacteristic girlish giggle and another sly wink, Rose left the apartment.

Terrific, Edie thought irritably. *Now Rose will be on my case every day trying to get all the juicy details of my romance with Mr. Hunk, Cliff Marchelli.* The whole idea of a love affair with Cliff was ludicrous. The man was about as lovable as a porcupine, and if he didn't shave soon he was going to resemble the creature, as well.

Still, she had to admit, there was a part of her that found Cliff intriguing. He gave of himself so stingily, exposing so little of the inner man. For every step forward she took to get to know him better, he took a step backward, guarding himself. The result was a macabre dance, back and forth, nobody leading, nobody following and nobody getting anywhere.

The thought of dancing caused her to jump out of the kitchen chair. She had reports to type and she wanted to wash her hair—so many things to do before this evening.

Five

_____

"Come on in." Edie opened the door to Cliff that evening. "I'll be out of your hair in just a few minutes."

"No problem," he replied, stepping into the apartment, his eyes perusing her from the top of her dark hair, over the simple black sheath she wore, down to the high-heeled silver shoes on her dainty feet.

"You're staring at me." She laughed self-consciously, a hand reaching up to twist the slender silver chain that adorned her neck.

"Sorry." He flushed and moved toward the window.

"Nanny is across the hall at Rose's and I'll probably be back home by ten-thirty, eleven at the latest." She looked at the silver wristwatch on her slender wrist. "Marcus should be here any time," she said more to herself than to him.

"Marcus?"

"Yes, Dr. Marcus Powers. He's the one taking me to the ballet." She looked at him curiously, seeing the deep frown that crinkled his brow. "Is there a problem?"

"Of course not," he replied brusquely, focusing his attention on his camera equipment. But of course there was a problem, and the problem was he hadn't considered that she might have a date for the evening. In his mind the scenario he'd envisioned had been different. He'd assumed she was going to the ballet with a bunch of female friends, women she had once worked with, or old schoolmates.

"Oh, there he is," she said, peering over his shoulder out the window. "Do I look all right?"

"You'll do," he said, his tone curt, not bothering to look up at her. No, you look too good to be going out in public. You should put up that hair and take down that short skirt. Those were the thoughts rolling around in his head as she grabbed a glittery silver purse from the table. "I'll see you later," she said.

He smiled wanly. "You'd better hurry. You don't want to keep him waiting."

She gazed at him for a long moment, then with a whisper of her scent as she passed by him, she disappeared out the door.

Cliff's gaze immediately sought the sidewalk below. He watched as Edie and the doctor hurried across the street toward the late-model foreign sports car parked there. Of course he'd have a sports car, to match the trendy image he presented in his shiny Italian suit. *And he probably wears colored bikini underwear,* he thought sourly. Anyone named Marcus would. Dr. Marcus Powers. Cliff abhorred the man already.

The sports car roared off, carrying Edie and the eminent doctor to the ballet. *And he probably speaks French and wears a pinkie ring.* For some reason these thoughts made depression settle around his shoulders like an old, familiar sweater.

He sighed deeply, suddenly realizing how silent the apartment was, as if when Edie had left she had taken all the life with her. He looked at his watch. She'd said she'd be home by ten-thirty, eleven at the latest. Four hours. He sat and watched the second hand on his wristwatch slowly making its revolutions. Four hours. He sighed, somehow knowing it was going to be the longest four hours of his life.

Moments later he got up and stretched. He went into the bathroom and swished cold water on his face, trying not to think of how utterly alluring Edie had looked for her date with the good doctor. As he left the bedroom he paused at the door to Edie's bedroom. Had it been completely closed, he would never have entered. As it was, the half-open door beckoned to him like an engraved invitation to a special party.

It was with the seasoned eyes of a cop that he examined the room, but it was the heart of a man that translated his impressions to personal terms.

Her room immediately told him several things. The floral wallpaper and ruffled bedspread said that the occupant was female. The single bed proclaimed a person accustomed to sleeping alone. A stack of books on the floor spoke of a quiet existence. These first impressions were filed and cataloged immediately due to his years of police experience.

Edie's room. Her presence was everywhere, from the bold, bright colors that breathed life into the room, to the subtle floral scent of her that lingered in the air. These perceptions were not those of a cop, but rather those of a man.

He walked over to her dressing table, unsurprised to find very little makeup cluttering the surface. Of course she didn't wear a lot of makeup. She didn't need it. His hand lingered over a bottle of perfume, fighting an impulse to open it and see if it contained the attractive scent he'd come to think of as hers alone. He left the bottle alone, preferring to believe that the scent didn't come from an artificial source, but simply emanated naturally from her skin. He felt a tightening of his loins as he saw the peach-colored wisp of silk that lay at the foot of the bed and remembered the way she had looked in the lingerie.

The blood pounded through him as he remembered the way her eyes had changed from the light brown of rich oak to a deep walnut when he'd kissed her. Her hair had been liquid mahogany, spilling over his hands. With a muttered oath he grabbed the slip of silk and threw it across the room, disgusted with himself and his pitiful fantasies.

He left her room, went back into the living room and sat in his chair at the window, his hand shaking slightly as he ran it through his thick hair. "I'm not right for her," he whispered, then added perversely, "but neither is that sports-car-driving doctor." He looked at his watch, then stared stonily out the window.

The ballet was wonderful. The scenery was breathtaking and the costumes stunning. It was one of the best productions of *Giselle* Edie had ever seen. Marcus was his usual charming self, but by the time intermission arrived, Edie was perfectly miserable. Several times during the first half of the performance she found herself drifting away from the tragedy of Giselle and into thoughts of Cliff.

He was the most complicated, frustrating man she'd ever known in her life. He had the amazing ability to crawl beneath her skin and lodge there like an irritating chigger.

There was no denying he'd frightened her with his kiss. What frightened her was that she'd found his kiss so exciting, so bewildering. She'd consciously tried to stay away from him for the past two days, but she hadn't been able to maintain the distance.

She now watched as Marcus made his way across the lobby of the large theater. He was so easy to understand. So why did her thoughts keep returning to the perplexing man back at her apartment?

"Here we are," Marcus said, smiling and handing her a glass of wine.

"Thank you," Edie murmured, stealing a glance at her watch. A few minutes after nine o'clock. She shoved the mental image of Cliff sitting in front of her window, in the dark, out of her mind and sipped her wine.

"Darling, is everything all right? You seem rather preoccupied this evening," Marcus said, his dark eyes filled with what looked to be concern.

"I'm sorry. I guess I'm just a little bit tired."

"Is Nanny keeping you up nights? Is she getting worse?"

Edie shook her head. "I don't know. Some days I think she's doing really well, then other days I wonder how much longer I'll be able to care for her at home. I know eventually I'll need to place her in a nursing home, and the thought just tears me apart." She didn't tell Marcus that there was another, equally disturbing reason for her sleepless nights.

Marcus leaned closer to her, engulfing her in a wave of expensive cologne. "I want you to put all these things out of your mind for the rest of the ballet. You're much too beautiful to have to worry about anything." He gazed deeply into her eyes.

For somebody who didn't know him well, the seductive purr of his words, his soulful gaze would have been enticing. But Edie knew how easily pretty words fell off Marcus's tongue, and she had a sneaking suspicion that whenever he gazed deeply into her eyes he was actually admiring his own reflection in her pupils.

"Marcus, you're a good friend." She touched his arm affectionately.

"Marry me and I'll take you away from all your worries," he said easily.

Edie laughed. "You know if I said yes, you'd totally freak out."

"Ah, Edie, you know me too well." He smiled ruefully. "Oh, look, there's Vivian and Bill." He waved at the friends approaching them. Edie stole another look at her watch, once again her mind filling with visions of Cliff.

"Marcus, thank you," Edie said much later as she and Marcus stopped in front of her apartment door. "I had a wonderful time and the performance was quite good."

"Yes, it was, wasn't it? I was particularly impressed with the young man who danced the role of the duke."

Edie nodded. "He was wonderful," she agreed.

He gazed at her affectionately. "You know, you're one of my favorite dates."

She laughed. "That's because you know I'm no threat. I don't make any demands on you."

"God forbid." He looked horrified. "Protect me from demanding women."

Edie laughed again and kissed him on his cheek. "Good night, Marcus."

"Good night, love. I'll call you later in the week."

She nodded, then slipped into the apartment, immediately spotting Cliff silhouetted in the darkness against the window. "Hi," she said softly, lighting the candle in the center of the table, illuminating the room with a soft glow.

He nodded. "Did you have a good time?"

She shrugged. "Sure, it was nice."

"It took you an awfully long time to say goodbye at the door."

"No more than usual."

"It seemed like a long time."

Edie turned and faced him, her hands on her hips. "You're much too young to be my father, and you don't look enough like me to be an overprotective big brother, so what's the deal?"

She saw his jaw clench tightly. "No big deal. I just wanted to make sure everything was all right."

"Everything is fine," she assured him, kicking off her high heels and flopping down on the sofa. "The ballet was wonderful. I've never seen so much talent on one stage." She put her feet up on the coffee table and wiggled her toes, thrilled to be out of the tight high heels.

"I suppose he's some kind of brilliant brain surgeon or a psychiatrist or something like that."

Edie's toes stopped wiggling. "Who?" She wondered if she had somehow missed part of the conversation.

"Dr. Powers." He remained looking out the window, his back rigidly straight. "I couldn't help but notice his fancy sports car. He must be some kind of really important doctor."

"Hmm, very important," she agreed with a hint of amusement in her voice. "He's a podiatrist."

"A what?" Cliff turned and looked at her.

"You know . . . a podiatrist, a foot doctor."

He stared at her a moment, then threw back his head and laughed. "A foot doctor?" His smile slowly faded. "Are you serious about this guy? I mean, are you involved with him?"

"Is this personal questioning a part of standard policy? You think because you're in my apartment that gives you a right to know my personal business?"

"Forget it. It was just a passing curiosity." He stared back out the window, angry with himself for even broaching the subject. But he hadn't been able to help himself. He'd seen the little sports car pull up out front, watched as Edie and the doctor had run across the street and into the building. He'd heard their murmurings and the sound of her soft laughter through the door, and found himself wondering if she was kissing the doctor good-night. He frowned. What did he care how Edie felt about Dr. Bunion?

"For the sake of passing curiosity, the answer is no. I'm not involved with Marcus. We're friends, good friends, and we occasionally share an evening out together."

Cliff's breath whooshed out of him in relief. He wasn't sure why, but he couldn't stand the thought of Edie involved with the slick doctor. "Speaking of feet, how's yours?" He turned toward her.

"A little tender, but okay. You must have gotten out all the glass."

"Good," he answered, trying not to think of how soft her leg had been, how much he had enjoyed caressing it. "Oh, by the way, I met your neighbor this morning. I think I might have given her the wrong impression."

"Yes, Rose thinks you and I are an item," Edie replied, snorting indelicately. "As if I could get interested in a man who keeps everything bottled up inside and spends all his money on junk food and antacid pills.''

"And I couldn't tolerate a woman who wouldn't let me eat a rare steak or a greasy cheeseburger.''

"And heaven forbid I ever become involved with a man who obviously doesn't own or know how to operate a razor.''

"And the devil take me if I ever hook up with a woman who vents her anger like a blast of dynamite.''

"I do not,'' Edie protested.

"Yes, you do.'' He turned back around and looked out the window once again, a grin stretched across his face. "You squawk and crow like an angry hen, slamming doors and letting everyone know within a ten-mile radius that Edith Turner is mad.''

"I most certainly do not,'' she exclaimed indignantly.

"Hey!'' Cliff yelped as a throw pillow hit him in the back of his head. He turned and grinned at her, rubbing his scalp. "You Turner women have the damnedest way of sneaking up and attacking a man from behind.''

She got up off the sofa and walked over to him. "And if you aren't very careful, you're going to make me forget why I was in such a hurry to get home from the ballet.'' With this she strode regally into her bedroom and slammed the door.

Cliff slowly shook his head, knowing he'd managed to make her mad once again. But for the life of him, as her final words played and replayed in his mind, he had a hell of a time wiping the silly grin off his face.

* * *

Hours later as the morning sun streaked the sky, Cliff stood and stretched. All night long he'd been haunted by visions of Edie sleeping in the next room. She'd been restless, too. He'd heard her up only moments before.

He packed up his equipment, lingering, hoping to see her before he left. When he was finished and she still hadn't come out of her bedroom, he decided to knock on the door and tell her he was going.

"Come in," she called, as if expecting the knock on her bedroom door.

Cliff pushed open the door and his breath caught in his throat. She stood at the window, clad in the peach-colored nightie that had tormented him since the morning he'd first seen her in it.

The early-morning sunlight whispered in her window, clinging to her skin and painting it a lush gold, playing in her hair and teasing out auburn glints. "I . . . I . . ." Whatever it was he meant to say was lost, swallowed by a heat of desire so intense it weakened his knees.

The knock on the door hadn't surprised Edie. She believed it was simply an extension of her own thoughts, a fulfillment of what she'd been wishing. She moved to him, not thinking of consequences, not contemplating what her action would bring, knowing only that it was right he was here with her now.

She saw the torment on his face, saw the battle going on within him. She placed her palms on both sides of his face and drew him toward her. "Yes," she breathed, and that single word seemed to decide his battle for him. With a moan he grabbed her to him, his lips plundering hers with an intensity that stole her breath away.

She folded herself into him, pressing her body against his, realizing he was already fully aroused. This knowledge only served to heighten her own desire. His hands stroked through her hair, across her shoulders, then moved down her back to cup her buttocks.

His lips moved from her mouth and she dropped her head back, allowing them access to her throat. At the same time her fingers deftly worked at the buttons of his shirt, wanting to feel the warmth of his naked flesh. He moaned as her hands laid claim to his chest, and he kissed her face, her throat, her lips, with his whiskers rubbing erotically against her skin.

She gasped as he pushed the delicate straps of her teddy off her shoulders, causing the flimsy piece of material to pool on the floor at their feet. With one swift movement he picked her up and carried her to the bed. He deposited her there gently, then stepped back and looked down at her, his eyes burning like those of a man fevered with illness. "Edie... if we go on, I won't be able to stop." His breathing was ragged and harsh. "You have to understand, no strings, no promises. Just this moment in time."

She reached up and took his hand and laid it on her breast. "You talk too much," she whispered up at him, her hand reaching out and touching the taut material of his jeans.

Her touch broke the last vestige of control Cliff claimed. He tugged off his jeans, kicked his briefs aside and joined her on the bed, wanting to possess her, own her completely.

Her skin was hot and as his hand moved across her breasts, down the flat surface of her stomach and to the center of her, the heat grew more intense, surrounding him, consuming him. His mouth found her breasts, his tongue licking her nipples, drawing them in and out of his lips. He loved the taste of her, the feel of her. He was caught in the sensation of the moment, captured in this single point in time. And as he moved between her thighs and plunged into her velvety softness, he knew that this moment had been inevitable since the first time he'd seen her.

Edie pulled him into her, needing him, reveling in the strength of his embrace, the pulsating warmth within her. She matched his rhythm as if they had made love a dozen times before, their bodies perfectly synchronized to their internal needs.

She gasped his name over and over again as she felt herself reaching...climbing for the white-hot burst of pleasure she knew was there. As she reached it, feeling it spill its shimmering light upon her, he cried out her name and relaxed on top of her, his warmth surrounding her completely.

For a long moment they didn't speak. Their bodies remained united, but she felt him drifting, distancing himself from her. "Cliff?" She breathed his name tentatively.

He rolled off her and out of the bed, reaching for his underwear. He pulled them on and quickly added his jeans, his gaze carefully averted from her. As he got into his shirt, he looked at her, his eyes dark and unfathomable. "This was a mistake, Edie." He held up a hand to still her protest. "It was a grave mistake and it won't happen again. The best thing to do is just pretend it didn't happen." He didn't wait for her answer. He turned and left the room and before Edie could get out of bed she heard the slam of her apartment door and knew he was gone.

Six

"**W**ould you like to stay for breakfast?"

Cliff looked at her in surprise. She'd surprised him a few minutes earlier by coming out of her bedroom wide awake and fully dressed. It had been two nights since her date with Marcus . . . two nights since they'd made love. He'd hardly seen her since then, hadn't spoken to her at all. She'd scurried to her bedroom when he arrived for surveillance, and in the mornings he ran out the door before she got up.

He now hesitated, torn between the desire to linger and an underlying fear that he was becoming too involved with the Turner family.

"Buttermilk pancakes with real maple syrup," she enticed with a smile.

He wasn't sure whether it was the promise of pancakes or her smile, but his fear suddenly seemed trivial. She'd obviously been able to put what had happened between them behind her. Surely he could do the same. "Okay, sounds great." He picked up his chair and carried it from the window to the table, watching her as she worked. She moved with a graceful efficiency, lining up ingredients on the counter like a mad scientist preparing a powerful potion. He smiled as she mixed the ingredients and began hand-beating the pancake batter. Her motion made her long braid swing hypnotically across her back, and her fanny jiggle invitingly. Suddenly he was hungry for more than just pancakes.

He jumped up from his chair. "Is there something I can do to help?"

"You can set the table." She pointed to the cabinet that held the plates. As she poured the batter in dollops onto the hot skillet, she watched Cliff out of the corner of her eyes.

He moved with the restless energy of a caged animal, concentrating intensely on getting the table set properly. She smiled as he chewed his bottom lip, meticulously folding the paper napkins and placing them carefully beneath each fork. He looked so appealing, like a young boy whose sole attention was focused on assembling a prized model airplane.

Suddenly she was overwhelmed by his presence, not the presence of an appealing boy but rather that of an attractive man. The flannel shirt he wore pulled taut across his upper body, emphasizing his broad shoulders and slender waist. His jeans loved the length of his legs and as he turned his back to her she remembered the way his skin had felt against her own, the way his body had fit so perfectly against her. She flipped the pancakes over, allowing her imagination free rein. She closed her eyes, enjoying the direction of her thoughts. Cliff coming up behind her and wrapping his arms around her, breathing butterfly kisses on the nape of her neck as she tried to finish up breakfast. Him telling her to forget the pancakes as he swept her up in his arms and whisked her into the bedroom, where she was lost in the dark burning of his eyes. She began to sizzle with the heat of her memories, the anticipation of her fantasies.

"Uh...do you always cook your pancakes until they're that interesting shade of black?"

"Huh?" His voice pulled her back to reality. As his words penetrated her brain, she looked down to see the pancakes smoking, their edges blackened and crispy. "Damn," she muttered, quickly transferring them from the skillet to the trash can. She'd believed it was her thoughts sizzling; instead it had been their breakfast. "I—I guess I dozed off for just a minute," she said with a flush, quickly pouring more batter on the hot skillet.

"Actually, I was sort of surprised to see you so wide awake and dressed this morning," he said, repositioning himself in a chair at the now perfectly set table. "Normally you stumble out of the bedroom like a robot whose circuits are not quite connecting."

She decided to ignore his last comment and instead explained. "I always get up and around early on Saturday mornings. Rose comes over and sits with Nanny and I go to the city market and do some shopping. Want to come with me?'' The invitation was issued purely on impulse. ''Never mind, I'm sure you're tired.'' She smiled apologetically. ''I forgot that while I sleep you're out here doing your job.'' She wanted to grab him, make him talk about what they had shared two nights earlier, but she knew nothing would make him run farther faster, and so she decided to play the game the way he wanted, pretending they hadn't shared a night of desire.

''I'd like to come with you if the offer still stands.'' Cliff's answer was just as impulsive as her question had been. Of course, it had nothing to do with wanting to spend time with her, sharing a couple of hours of the day in her company. ''I've never been to the city market before,'' he added, as if this was the sole reason for him wanting to come.

''Oh, it's wonderful. It's the best place to go for fresh fruits and vegetables. But that's not all they sell. There's clothing, perfume, animals, house plants…it's like an open-air department store.''

''Sounds fascinating.'' But he was actually thinking how fascinatingly beautiful she looked, with her eyes sparkling like chunks of topaz and a cheek decorated with a speckle of pancake batter. The jeans she wore were worn and faded, conforming to her body with familiarity. Was it possible to be jealous of a pair of jeans? he mused. The russet-colored sweater she had on brought out the auburn glints in her dark hair. He tore his gaze away from her and studiously re-folded one of the napkins on the table. He didn't want to think about her loveliness. He didn't want to linger on thoughts of her heated flesh, the feel of her moist femininity surrounding him.

"Okay, if you just sit tight, I'll get Nanny and we'll eat," Edie said, flipping the last of the pancakes onto a large platter.

Within minutes they were all sitting at the table, the early-morning autumn sun spilling into the window to fill the kitchen with cheerful sunshine. Edie kept up a steady stream of meaningless chatter. She ate her pancakes the way she seemed to do everything, with enthusiastic gusto. Nanny refused to eat the pancakes, insisting that she had eaten a full breakfast earlier in the day, but she smiled benignly, occasionally patting first Edie's hand, then Cliff's.

The scene was seductive to him, like the wholesome quality of a Norman Rockwell painting. Husband, wife, grandmother...all that was missing was a chubby baby in a high chair drooling syrup down double chins. Yes, the scene pulled at something that had been buried deep within him—a longing, a wistful desire to belong to someone, to share with someone. The scene whispered of caring, promised permanence. But he wasn't fooled. He knew there was no such thing as permanence, that like a mirage of water in a sand-blown desert, if he tried to grab it in his hand it would disappear.

They had just finished eating when Edie jumped as a knock sounded on the door. "That will be Rose."

"Good morning, love." Rose's eyes lit up at the sight of Cliff. "Ah...Mr. Marchelli, another early-morning visit."

"Cliff's coming with me to the city market," Edie explained, ignoring the look of utter delight on Rose's face. "We'll be out of here in just a minute or two." She began to clear off the table.

"Just leave those," Rose demanded, taking the plates from Edie's hands. "Nanny and I can clean up the dishes. You two run along and enjoy the morning." She looked at them expectantly. "Well, go on, get out of here."

Edie and Cliff didn't hesitate, but headed for the door. "Anything you need?" Edie asked before they left.

"Get me a couple of nice zucchini," Rose instructed.

Edie nodded, closing the apartment door behind her.

"She's something else," Cliff said with a laugh as they walked down the stairs.

As they stepped out into the brisk morning air, Cliff stretched and took a deep, cleansing breath.

"Are you sure you aren't too tired?" She looked at him worriedly.

"No." He stretched again with hands overhead, the motion pulling his shirt from the waistband of his pants, exposing firm, tanned skin covered with crisp, dark hairs. Edie averted her eyes and quickened her pace. "It usually takes a couple of hours for me to unwind."

She nodded, still flustered by that sight of his flesh.

"You want me to take my car?" he asked. "It's parked just across the street. I could drive us." He hurried to catch up with her as she moved quickly down the sidewalk.

"Oh, no, part of the fun of living this close to the city market is walking there, then trying to get back home with all the treasures you've bought."

"Oh, I see. You invited me along so I could serve as your pack mule," he teased.

She nodded. "It's true, you found me out. I was so pleased when the police decided to send an officer to set up surveillance in my apartment, because I knew that some Saturday morning I would be going to the city market and I would need that officer along to carry my purchases. I confess, you're too smart for me." Her sparkling eyes belied the solemn tones of her voice.

Cliff threw back his head and laughed, glad he had agreed to come with her. He decided at that moment that he was going to enjoy the morning. He wasn't going to think of the past or the future. He simply wanted to savor this moment in time, with this particular woman.

Edie wasn't sure exactly what made the change in him, but suddenly he looked younger, more relaxed. His eyes no longer held the dark, brooding quality she'd come to expect. Instead they glowed with anticipation, and she wanted to do whatever she could to keep them that way.

"Come on." She grabbed his hand and tugged him along as the stalls of the city market came into view. Immediately the air was filled with the pungent scent of ripe vegetables and fruit, mingling with the smells of hot pretzels, pizza and grilled hot dogs. Crowds of people milled around, their voices filling the early morning.

"Hey, Vinnie, how's Maria?" Edie greeted the vendor in the first stall they approached.

The young Italian man gave her a brilliant smile. "Fat as a cow. The doctor says any day now."

"You be sure and let me know." She turned to Cliff. "Maria is pregnant and everyone in the neighborhood is anxiously awaiting the event. She and Vinnie have four little girls and they're hoping this one is going to be a boy."

"Don't doctors have tests that tell parents what to expect?"

"Oh, pooh, why take all the fun out of it," she scoffed, tugging him along to the next stall.

As they moved from booth to booth, Cliff wasn't surprised that she greeted most of the vendors by name and they all seemed to know her. Many of them asked about Nanny, telling Edie to give the older woman their regards.

He watched in amusement as Edie picked over the vegetables like a miner looking for a gold nugget. "You're really into this vegetarian stuff, aren't you?" he observed as she paid for several large green peppers.

"I'm not fanatical about it. It's just a conscious decision I've made," she explained as they walked through the throng of people. "I've never been much of a meat lover, so it really wasn't a huge sacrifice. Besides, Nanny is getting more and more difficult when it comes to mealtime. She either insists she's already eaten, or simply doesn't want to eat. When I can get her to, I want to make sure it's the healthiest, most nutritious meal I can fix, so I've gone to mostly vegetable dishes.''

"But eating meat wouldn't hurt her, would it?" he asked. "Surely you could give her a taco every now and again."

"I suppose so." It pleased her that he worried about Nanny getting her precious tacos. Funny, he seemed so determined to give the impression that he never did anything nice for anyone. Yet he'd remembered an old woman's craving for tacos. She wasn't sure who he was trying to fool with his macho posturings, but he certainly wasn't fooling her.

"Oh, Cliff, look at the strawberries." Her attention was captured by stacked flats of the plump, red berries. "I can't believe they have such wonderful strawberries this late in the year."

She grabbed a huge one, pulled off the stem and popped it into her mouth, giggling as juice squirted out of the corner and dribbled down her chin.

Cliff's breath caught in his throat as he gazed at her. She was so damned beautiful. Tendrils of hair escaped from the braid, curling around her face and clinging to her neck. The brisk autumn air had caused pink circles to appear on her cheeks, and the berry juice stained her lips a bright crimson.

"Cliff, you really should taste one. They're so sweet."

He wanted to taste, all right. He wanted to take his tongue and run it slowly from her chin up to her ruby lips, capturing the sweet strawberry juice that lingered there. He wanted to repeat the experience they'd shared. The thought made his knees weaken and threaten to buckle. He was vaguely conscious of the people surrounding them, the amazed gaze of the watching vendor. He knew he couldn't follow through on his first impulse, so he did the next best thing. He took his index finger and slowly moved it up her chin, across her ruby lips, gently swiping at the sweet berry juice, then he transferred his finger to his mouth. "Hmm, it is sweet." His voice was a husky rumble.

Time seemed to stand still for Edie. The surroundings of the city market and the people seemed to fade away as she found herself trapped in the depths of desire. Raw eroticism . . . his finger slowly trailing across her lips, then moving to his own mouth. The action had caused a welling of emotion so intense it disoriented her.

"You like the strawberries? For you, I'll knock a dollar off the price of a flat."

Edie looked at the vendor blankly, as if he was speaking a foreign language. "Huh?"

"We'll take a flat," Cliff said smoothly, reaching into his back pocket for his wallet.

By the time Cliff had completed the transaction for the berries, Edie had herself back under control. For the next two hours they sniffed melons, squeezed oranges and inspected for lumps, bumps and bruises. They selected Rose's zucchini and Edie bought summer squash, green beans and a sack of new potatoes. They laughingly organized and reorganized their purchases, wishing for more hands or a shopping basket or two.

Cliff watched with amused indulgence as she oohed in delight over the live rabbits, quacked back at the caged ducks and squealed in horror when a vendor offered her a taste of squid. He was disappointed when she suggested it was time to go home.

"I told you I should have driven the car," he grumbled, balancing the flat of strawberries in one arm and a dozen other sacks in his other. "Before we begin this trek back to your apartment, I need sustenance." He pointed to the corner restaurant across from the marketplace.

"It hasn't been that long ago that you had a plateful of pancakes," she protested with a laugh.

"Yes, but even pack mules get a lump of sugar or a carrot before making a long trip with a heavy load," he wheedled with a boyish grin.

She relented. "Okay, okay." Besides, she was reluctant to have the shopping trip end. She knew when they got back to her apartment he would go home, and she was enjoying his company far too much to want the morning to be finished. He was a different man today, a man fighting shadows instead of dwelling in them. And she saw what he would be like if those shadows were banished forever. It was a promising image.

"What would you like?" he asked once they were settled in a booth at the back of the small restaurant.

"Just a cup of tea. I'm really not hungry."

"Are you sure? I think I'm going to have the Mexican omelet."

She frowned at him, concern darkening her eyes. "Do you have a death wish, or what?"

"What do you mean?"

She looked at him patiently. "It's obvious you have ulcers, painful ones that keep you eating those antacid tablets. Yet you continue to eat junk that only makes you suffer more."

"But I like spicy food."

"And I like to take midnight walks, but I'm smart enough to realize that midnight walks in this neighborhood are dangerous. When are you going to realize that spicy foods are harmful to you?"

"Speaking of the danger of midnight walks, why are you and Nanny still living in this part of the city?"

She knew he was purposely changing the subject and she flashed him a knowing grin. "I thought about moving Nanny into the apartment where I lived at the time she got ill, but then decided to move in with her and take over the responsibilities of landowner."

"Why don't you just sell the building? You could probably see a decent profit." Cliff studied her curiously.

"Oh, I couldn't." She looked at him, horrified at the thought. "All the tenants are elderly, living on fixed incomes. Most of them have been in those apartments for the last twenty years, still paying their original amount of rent. There's Mrs. Catrell on the third floor—she's ninety years old and has no family. Then there's Mr. Williams on one—he's confined to a wheelchair. Where would they go? How could they afford to move?" She broke off as the waitress appeared at their table.

"The lady would like a cup of tea, and I'll have two eggs over easy, toast and a glass of milk." He smiled at Edie. "Better?"

She nodded, reaching across the table and touching his hand. "Much better. I don't want to have to worry about you."

His eyes darkened slightly and he pulled his hand away from hers. "Don't worry about me. What happened the other night—it doesn't give you the right... I don't want your concern."

"My concern is just that—my concern—and I can give it to anyone I want to," she returned lightly. She knew she was losing him. She could see the shadows of darkness drawing in on him, pulling his facial features tensely, making his shoulders more rigid. Part of her wanted to pull him to her breast, stroke his brow and tell him everything would be all right. But there was a perverse part of her that wanted to dig deeply into his psyche, find the shadowmaker that resided there and purge it from his soul forever. She decided to follow her instincts and dig. "Tell me about your wife."

His eyes widened, then the light in them was swallowed in darkness and a muscle began to jump rhythmically in his clenched jaw. "There's nothing to tell. She left me two years ago."

"How long were you married?"

Cliff looked beyond her, his eyes distant and full of anger... pain... bitterness, a myriad of emotions playing across their dark surface. "Three years. We dated for three months and she started talking about getting married. At first I wasn't interested. I didn't believe in permanence. My parents' 'happily ever after' lasted until I was ten years old, then my father walked out on us. I didn't have much faith in commitment and fairy-tale endings.'' He laughed bitterly and refocused his attention on Edie, the bitterness in his eyes making her shiver uncontrollably. ''But Catherine was persistent, and her love was powerful, and she finally made me believe that we had a future together.'' He laughed again, a cruel, harsh sound. ''Yeah, we had a future together—three whole years. Then she walked out and left me. She took the life from me.''

He was angry, but he was unsure exactly where his anger should be directed. Edie was an easy target, sitting across from him, her eyes huge with his pain. Yet his anger wasn't directed just at her. Sure, he was mad because she had dug into his life, picking at the scabs of his past. But he was also angry with fate. Like a miser who shows a peek of his coveted gold, then firmly shuts the safe door, fate had shown him a glimpse of happiness, then snatched it away. Catherine had shown him what it was to love and be loved, then had left him alone forever.

''Oh, Cliff,'' Edie breathed tremulously, knowing nothing she could say could diminish the heartache that blackened his life. Yet in the same moment she was experiencing the pain of his loss, she was also feeling the wonder of a very different emotion. This pain in his life, his loss of faith in anything lasting—it was the final piece to the perplexing puzzle that he presented to her. It explained so many different things. ''Cliff, I'm sorry. I didn't mean to—'' She broke off and looked down at the top of the table. "I was going to say I didn't mean to pry, but that isn't true. I did want to pry. I wanted to know about you and your past, the people who have been important to you." She looked up at him once again, searching his face, looking for forgiveness in his angry features. "We've had a nice morning, I feel close to you, and I wanted to know...I needed to understand...." She looked at him helplessly.

He tried to maintain his anger. Anger was such a clean, simple emotion and there was comfort in the familiarity of it. But as he looked at her his anger ran like a cowardly comrade in the face of battle. Without his rage he felt himself experiencing a new, very different emotion—relief. He didn't stop to analyze this new feeling. "Edie, before the other night, I hadn't been with a woman since Catherine. I took advantage of you." He studied her for a long moment. "Don't make it into anything other than what it was, an explosion of physical need."

Although his words caused a tickle of pain in Edie's heart, she nodded slowly. He'd been hurt, and she had a feeling his words were generated from that hurt. But when he'd held her in his arms it had been her name he'd called out, her eyes he'd gazed into. Although Cliff's lips said one thing, his body language had spoken something quite different to her, and it was this she clung to.

"Good," he said. "Now, can we please leave this particular subject alone?"

They tried to recapture the friendship, the laughter they had shared at the city market, but like an elusive butterfly the warmth was gone, the earlier kinship shattered by the intrusion of his past and their moment of passion.

As Cliff ate his eggs and she sipped her tea, the conversation stayed neutral. They talked about how the neighborhood had changed, how much Kansas City was growing.

"In another couple of days your face will be the proud owner of an official beard," she said with a smile.

"How can you tell the difference between an official beard and a face full of whiskers?" he asked, pushing his now-empty plate away from him.

Without thought, Edie reached across the table and gently stroked his face, running her finger lightly from his temple down to his chin. "Whiskers are rough and scratchy, but a beard is soft." Her finger lingered on his chin, achingly close to his bottom lip.

He shuddered at her touch, his eyes hungry and full of fire. He recoiled suddenly, his hand shooting up to grab her wrist and pull it away from his face. He'd told her that making love to her had been a mistake, one that wouldn't be repeated. "Are you ready to go?" He released her hand, his eyes darkly inscrutable.

She nodded and rose from the table with him. He could shutter his eyes against her, hide beneath them like the fearful hiding behind shades pulled tightly closed, but she'd seen the greedy blaze that had ignited in the depths of his eyes at her touch, and she knew with a certainty that as much as he protested, he was not untouched by her.

Their walk back to the apartment building was leisurely, not by choice but because they were encumbered with all their purchases.

"I'll make a deal with you," he said, hefting the flat of strawberries up on his shoulder like a busboy carrying a tray of dirty dishes.

"What?"

"I'll leave this flat of strawberries for you and Nanny if you'll put a bowl of them on the kitchen table for me to munch on at night."

She smiled up at him. "Does this mean you're giving up your late-night snacks of barbecue potato chips and Twinkies?"

He looked at her in surprise. "How do you know what I eat in the middle of the night?"

"I'm a good detective," she answered smugly, then laughed. "And your wrappers are always on top of the garbage can in the mornings."

She laughed as they trudged up the stairs to the apartment. Before they could go inside, Rose flung open the door, a finger to her lips as she hissed for them to be quiet. "Nanny's sleeping," she whispered. "Why don't you go back out for another hour or so? Get some fresh air and take advantage of my being here." She started grabbing bags from them, setting them just inside the door.

"Rose, you don't have to stay here any longer. I'm sure you have other things to do today," Edie protested, not wanting to take advantage of her goodwill.

"All I have to do is clean, and I've got every day for the rest of my life to do that." She took the flat of strawberries from Cliff. "Now, you two get back out there and enjoy the beautiful fall day. Before you know it snow will be flying and you'll be wishing for a day like today." She closed the door in their faces.

"I somehow feel like I've just been thrown out of my own house," Edie said.

"I think you have." Cliff grinned, then continued. "But she's right, you know. You really should take advantage of the time to yourself."

They walked back outside into the warmth of the midmorning sun. "What are you going to do now? We've already bought out the city market."

"I think I'll just take a walk. Rose is right, we won't have many more mild days. But you probably want to go home and get some sleep," she added. "Don't worry about me. I'm used to being on my own."

"I think I've gotten my second wind. I'm really not a bit tired." He smiled at her. "Want some company on your walk?"

"I'd love your company," she answered simply, then smiled enigmatically. "Come on, I've got a special place to show you." She grabbed his hand, hurrying him along.

They passed the city market and its booths, and the warehouses that lined the Missouri River bank. "Edie, where are you taking me?" he protested as she led him closer and closer to the swirling river water.

"Just follow me," she said with a laugh as they walked in single file along the edge of the river.

"I know, you're bringing me down here to drown me," he exclaimed.

"Ha, don't tempt me," she flung back over her shoulder with a wide grin.

After just a few minutes of walking they came to an area where the bank of the river was fairly low. In the river, an easy jump from land, was a large, flat rock protruding out of the water. Edie jumped to the rock, then beckoned for Cliff to join her. Once he was on the rock with her, she sat down, drew her knees up to her chest and smiled up at him.

"This is my fishin' and a-wishin' rock." She waited until he was seated beside her, then continued. "I spent much of my childhood right here."

"You used to come here as a child? Wasn't that pretty dangerous?" He eyed the swiftly swirling water that surrounded them.

"When I was little I didn't think it was dangerous. It wasn't until I got older that I realized it would have been easy to fall into the river."

"I can't imagine Nanny allowing you to come down here."

Edie laughed. "Nanny would have skinned me alive if she'd known I was here. Nanny's number-one rule was to stay away from the river."

"So you were a rebellious child, ignoring the rules," he teased.

"Not really," she returned. "Only the rules I thought were silly ones." She raised her face to the warmth of the sun. "This rock was like a magical place drawing me back to it again and again." She smiled wistfully, but didn't open her eyes. "I'd come here and talk to my parents. Somehow I thought that if I was sitting on my magical rock, wherever they were, they could hear me." She cracked an eyelid and smiled ruefully. "Crazy, the things we come up with when we're kids."

"But it must have been hard on you, losing your parents at such an early age." His gaze on her was serious.

Edie shrugged. "I suppose loss is hard, no matter how old you are. But you should know about that. You were young when your parents divorced." She looked at him, enjoying the way the sun played on the darkness of his hair and emphasized the lines and angles of his strong face.

"I was ten." The starkness of his voice told her much more than a long dissertation on the subject ever could.

She sat quietly, not wanting to pry as she had earlier at the restaurant, but wanting him to tell her only what he was comfortable in sharing.

He was silent for a moment. The only noise was the whoosh of the swiftly moving water that lapped at the rock, and an occasional splash as a fish broke the surface. "I didn't even know he and my mom were having problems." His voice was so low that Edie had to lean forward slightly to hear him. "One day Dad was there, and the next day he left for work and never came home. I can remember the day very clearly, because Dad had promised he'd take me to a ball game. After school I got my mitt and baseball hat and sat on the front porch, waiting for him to get home. Mom told me he wouldn't be coming, but I didn't believe her. After all, he'd promised me. I sat and waited for him until long after dark, then finally realized he wasn't coming."

All the while Cliff talked, he was looking off into the distance. Edie's heart constricted tightly in her chest as she thought of him as a little boy, mitt in hand, waiting for somebody who had never come. "It must have been painful for you," she said softly.

He straightened his shoulders, as if physically shrugging off the burden of old memories. "So, tell me. Have you ever caught fish here?"

"Never," she confessed. "I'd sit here for hours with my pole in the water and I never even had a nibble."

"Why'd you keep coming back?" he asked curiously.

"I don't know. Stubborn, I guess." She hugged her knees more closely to her chest and raised her face once again to the sun. "You have to admit, it's a very peaceful place, a good place to reflect on the complexities of life."

Cliff laughed. "And that's what you did when you were young? Come here and reflect on the complexities of life?"

"Sure."

"What kind of complexities can a kid have to reflect on?"

"Oh, you know, the usual things." She grinned at him. "How far is infinity, is there really a heaven, things like that."

"Oh, you mean the plaguing little questions that have stumped philosophers and scientists for centuries."

"Exactly. I also wondered why Jimmy Mayfield kissed with his mouth open."

"And just who, exactly, is this bold Jimmy Mayfield?" he asked teasingly.

"Jimmy Mayfield was my boyfriend in second grade. I brought him here to my special rock for the momentous occasion of my first kiss. And that kiss totally grossed me out."

"Are you in the habit of bringing the men in your life to your special rock?"

Edie looked at him seriously. "You're the first person I've brought here since Jimmy."

He looked at her in surprise, strangely touched by her words. "Thanks for sharing your special place with me."

"You're welcome," she answered simply.

For the next few minutes they sat side by side, enjoying a solitude filled with their togetherness. Cliff was struck again by her beauty. It wasn't necessarily the beauty of her features, although any man would find her attractive. But more than that, her beauty came from an inward serenity. She seemed to be at peace with herself, and she had the gift of transmitting that peace to the people around her. She was easy to be with, like the river that surrounded them. She went with the flow, following the contours of life. Sure, there were occasional storms when, like the river, she swelled with rage, but the waters always receded, leaving behind the gentle, peaceful flow.

"Edie." He didn't even know what he wanted to say to her. He only knew he wanted to look into her doe eyes.

She turned and looked at him expectantly, and as he looked into her eyes, he knew he was going to kiss her and he knew he shouldn't, but he could no more stop himself than he could stop the age-old flow of the water around the rock. Without giving it another thought he leaned forward and tasted her lips with his.

This kiss had none of the violent intensity of the first kiss they had shared, nor had it the passion of their lovemaking. His lips played gently against hers, his tongue a welcomed intruder as it sought entry. Neither moved to deepen the kiss. They remained untouching except for the fusion of mouth against mouth.

Cliff broke the kiss, standing and brushing off the seat of his pants. "We'd better get back," he said, holding out his hand to help her up.

She nodded, reluctant to leave but knowing he was right. She took his hand and stood, pleased when he didn't drop her hand but continued to hold it as they walked slowly away from Edie's magical rock.

Seven

"I love fall, don't you?" Edie said as they walked slowly through the city market area. "The colorful leaves, hot cider, pumpkins on the vine."

He grinned at her. "You sound like a seasonal greeting card." He looked at her curiously. "Speaking of fall, what do you cook for Thanksgiving? A squash in the shape of a turkey?"

"No," Edie said with a laugh. "I must confess, that's one day when I throw away my vegetarian ways. We have turkey and stuffing and all the trimmings. It's a wild day. I cook for all the tenants in the building and we all get together in my apartment. Everyone eats too much and drinks too much, but there's a wonderful feeling of togetherness."

"Sounds nice." And it did. Cliff had spent the past two years of holidays working. He couldn't remember a holiday spent with people he liked.

Edie's smile slowly turned to one of puzzlement as she looked down the street toward her apartment building. "Something is going on at home." She quickened their pace, an unsettling feeling making her head pound with a sudden rush of adrenaline. Her heart jumped up in her throat as she caught sight of an ambulance pulling away from the curb, its siren splitting the air like the shrill cry of a baby in pain. A dark foreboding swept over her, making her jerk her hand away from Cliff's as she began running down the sidewalk.

"Edie!"

She was only barely conscious of Cliff calling after her. Terror jumped into her mouth, filling it with a vile taste as she saw Rose standing on the sidewalk, wringing her hands, fat tears streaming down her face.

"Rose." Edie's voice was a whisper as she touched the woman on the shoulder. "What happened?" She was vaguely aware of Cliff's presence beside her.

"Oh, Edie, it's all my fault. I should have been watching . . . but I thought she was sleeping. . . ." Sobs made her words nearly incoherent.

"Rose, slow down. Take a deep breath and tell us slowly." The authority in Cliff's voice made her do as she was told.

"I was in the bedroom, making up Nanny's bed. I looked out at her a couple of times, and she was sound asleep on the sofa." She bit her bottom lip and looked at Edie pleadingly. "I didn't know she woke up, but she must have wandered out into the hallway, and I heard her.... She fell down the stairs...."

"Oh, dear God." Edie's knees buckled and she swayed. She would have fallen had Cliff not grabbed her and pulled her tightly against him. She clung to him, his broad chest her anchor in the sea of fear that surrounded her.

"Where did they take her?" Cliff asked Rose, his arm tightening around Edie.

"North Kansas City Hospital." Rose burst into tears once again.

Edie raised a white, stricken face to Cliff. "Would you mind coming to the hospital with me?" She clung to his waist desperately.

He touched her cheek softly. "I wouldn't have it any other way." With his arm still firmly enclosing her, he led her to his car.

The ride to the hospital was accomplished in silence. Edie sat numbed with worry, afraid to speculate on Nanny's condition.

Cliff also was quiet. He saw the strain on Edie's face, knew the torture she must be in, but he didn't want to mouth meaningless platitudes or give her false hopes. Nanny was so frail, and he knew the danger of brittle bones. A fall down a flight of stairs could easily have tragic consequences.

Instead of talking, Cliff told Edie of his support by holding her hand. His enclosed hers on the car seat between them, his heart expanding as he felt her trembling, like a captured, frightened bird. He wanted to do more to comfort her, he wanted to tell her that everything would be all right, that Nanny was stronger than she appeared. What did other people say in situations such as these? There were times when his inability to articulate his innermost feelings was particularly frustrating.

They hurried to the hospital to wait. Edie filled out all the necessary papers, then they were instructed to have a seat in the emergency waiting room, that the doctor would be out to see them after he attended to Nanny.

"You want some coffee or something? We might have a long wait." Cliff paced restlessly as Edie sat in one of the molded plastic chairs. "I think I'll go down to the cafeteria and get a cup of coffee. What about you?"

"No, thanks, nothing for me." Her mouth moved in the semblance of a smile, but her face remained unnaturally pale. "But if you want something, go ahead."

He hesitated, torn between the need to escape the oppressive air of the waiting room and the desire to comfort her. "I'll be right back," he promised, hurrying to the elevator that would take him to the bottom floor and the cafeteria. He'd grab a cup of coffee and hurry back to her. She'd been strong so far, but her self-control could shatter at any moment, and if it did he wanted to be there to help her pick up the pieces.

Once he had left, Edie released a shuddery sigh, fighting the tears that pressed hotly against her eyelids. *Oh, Nanny,* she thought in despair. *I shouldn't have left you. I should have seen something like this coming.* She leaned forward in the chair, her hands covering her face as she said all the prayers she could think of. She didn't know how long she remained in this position—praying, begging, bargaining for Nanny to be all right.

"Edie, are you okay?"

She looked up at the sound of Cliff's voice, and for a moment, feeling his concern washing over her, she was okay. As she looked into his warm, worried brown eyes, she knew no matter what happened she would be all right.

"You spilled your coffee." She pointed to the dark stain on his pants just above his knee.

"I was in a hurry." He sat in the chair next to her and took a sip of the coffee. "You want a drink?"

She shook her head, her gaze going to the door where the doctor would emerge.

For several long moments they sat silently, Edie staring at the doorway and Cliff watching her, worrying about her.

He suddenly slammed the disposable coffee cup down on the end table, ignoring the dark liquid that sloshed over the sides of the cup. "What's taking so long?" He jumped up out of the chair as if it had become electrified. "Why doesn't somebody come out and tell us something?"

"I'm sure someone will tell us something as soon as they know something," she replied, although she had been wondering the same thing. "Why don't you sit down?"

"I can't sit down." Cliff ran a hand through his hair, pacing back and forth before her. He was confused, unsure what was causing his intense agitation. Was it the anticipation of a doctor walking through that door, resignation in his eyes as he told them in professional tones that Nanny was gone, or was it the fact that he suddenly realized that he cared about both Nanny and Edie? And it was a caring that scared the hell out of him.

They both jumped as a doctor appeared in the doorway.

"Dr. Stafford." Edie greeted the white-coated man by name, hurrying over to where he stood. Cliff immediately went to her side, placing an arm around her slender shoulders. He wanted to be her pillar, her strength should the news be bad. "How is she?" Edie's voice was a pained whisper, and Cliff tightened his grip on her.

"She'll be all right."

Edie sagged against Cliff, relief flowing off her in waves. "Thank God," she murmured.

"She's shaken up, rather badly bruised, and her collarbone has been fractured," the doctor explained.

"Where is she? Can we see her?"

Dr. Stafford nodded. "They're checking her in to room 202 right now. I want to keep her here for a day or two, keep her under observation. She took quite a spill." He looked at Edie kindly. "Perhaps it's time to start considering some of the alternatives we've discussed before."

She nodded slowly. "Yes, I suppose it is." Pain laced her voice. "Can we see her now?"

"Room 202. Don't stay too long, and I'll keep you informed should there be any changes in her condition."

It took only minutes for them to find the room. When they walked in, Edie's heart constricted as she looked at Nanny, lying so small and still in the large hospital bed.

"She's been given a sedative, so she'll be quite groggy," a nurse explained before leaving them alone in the room.

"Oh, Cliff," Edie breathed in dismay, moving to the side of the bed. There was a large bruise on Nanny's cheek and another on her forehead. Her neck and shoulder blade were immobilized by a thick, white strap. "Nanny." Edie took her grandmother's hands on hers. Nanny's eyes fluttered open and she stared at Edie for a long moment.

"Where am I? What am I doing here?" Nanny's voice quivered with fear.

"You're in the hospital. You had a fall, but you're fine now." Edie stroked her hand soothingly. "They're going to take care of you here for a few days."

"I don't want to stay here. I don't like it here." Nanny's lower lip trembled. "Would you please do me a favor?"

"Anything," Edie answered without hesitation.

"Call my granddaughter. Her name is Edith. She'll take care of me. She won't make me stay here."

Edie fought her impulse to fulfill Nanny's wish and whisk her out of the hospital. But she knew Nanny was where she needed to be.

"Edie would want you to stay here and let the doctors take care of you."

Nanny closed her eyes, as if wanting to escape her surroundings.

Edie turned as Cliff touched her on the shoulder. "Sleep is the best thing for her right now." His eyes were lit with compassion and once again Edie was struck by how much she had come to care for this man.

"Why don't you let me take you out for a late lunch?" he suggested as they walked out of the room.

"Lunch?" She looked at him blankly. Was it possible it was just lunchtime? It seemed like a lifetime ago that the three of them had sat at the kitchen table eating pancakes for breakfast. She frowned and looked back toward Nanny's door. "I don't know. Maybe I should stay here...just in case she needs me."

He placed his hands on her shoulders. "Edie, there's no reason for you to stay here. There's nothing you can do at the moment for Nanny. Besides, you heard the nurse, she's been given a sedative, so she'll probably sleep all afternoon." His hands gently massaged her tense shoulder muscles. "Come have lunch with me, then you can go home and nap for a couple of hours and come back here this evening. By that time Nanny will probably need to see you."

"Okay," she agreed, seeing the wisdom of his words. Now that the initial urgency and worry had passed, she was feeling tired and a little bit hungry. He was right, the best thing to do was go to eat and rest now, while Nanny was sedated.

"The first thing we are going to do is stop by my place and let me get a quick shower and a change of clothes," Cliff said once they were back in his car.

Edie nodded absently, preoccupied with thoughts of Nanny and the uncertainty of the future. Was it time to consider a nursing home? The thought tore at Edie's heart, yet she wanted to do what was best for her grandmother. Perhaps a residential care center, where Nanny could have her own room with all her familiar furnishings around her. Oh, it was all so confusing, and it was such a difficult decision to have to make. It was something she had hoped she wouldn't have to think about for a long time to come.

"Are you all right?" His words penetrated the confusion of her thoughts.

"I'm fine," she assured him. "I—I just wish I hadn't gone to the city market. I shouldn't have left her."

"Surely you aren't blaming yourself for what happened to Nanny." Cliff smoothly maneuvered the car into a parking space in front of the apartment complex. He shut off the car engine and turned to look at her. "Edie, accidents happen. We can't blame ourselves for what fate throws our way." A curious thing happened as Cliff spoke these words. The excess emotional baggage he'd been carrying around, the feeling that he'd somehow been responsible for Catherine's desire to leave him, exposed itself and melted away like snowflakes on a warm pane of glass. Funny, he hadn't even known those feelings were there until they were gone.

"Oh, logically I know I'm really not to blame. I guess I'm just dreading the decisions I know I'm going to have to make."

He smiled gently at her and smoothed an errant strand of hair off her cheek. "No decisions have to be made today. Nanny is going to be staying in the hospital for the next couple of days, so you don't need to make any future plans right now."

"You're absolutely right," she said in relief, feeling as if she had been given a reprieve from her unsettling thoughts.

"Come on, it will just take me a few minutes to shower and change, then I'm going to get you a good, hot plate of those vegetables you love so much." He grinned teasingly, getting out of the car.

"Nice complex," she observed as they walked across the parking lot.

"It's okay," he answered. "It's the place where I hang my hat, eat a few meals and sleep."

"Sounds like you're describing a hotel room rather than the place you live," Edie observed. But when Cliff led her into the apartment, that was exactly the way it looked—like an impersonal, cold hotel room.

The furniture looked new, an attractive plaid sofa and a recliner chair. The glass-topped end tables showed no signs of use, no rings from coffee cups, no newspapers or magazines cluttering the tops. The room emitted no warmth, no personality.

"Make yourself at home and I'll be out in just a few minutes," Cliff said, disappearing into what Edie presumed to be the bathroom.

"Can I use your phone? I want to call Rose and tell her Nanny is all right."

"Sure, it's in the kitchen." A moment later she heard the sound of water running in the shower.

Edie walked into the kitchen, unsurprised to find this room as impersonal as the living room. Sadness welled up in her heart for him. He was a man for whom heartache had stolen his lust for life. He merely existed through each day, afraid to expose himself, afraid to reach out for happiness and love, afraid of being hurt once again.

She had known him such a brief time and yet she felt as if she'd known him forever. And she knew with the certainty of a woman in love that there was a part of Cliff rebelling against his self-imposed isolation. There was a part of him that yearned for a connection with somebody. His mouth spoke protection, pushing her away with macho words and imposing sneers, but his eyes spoke of his need to be loved and to love. She knew there was a struggle going on inside him. She knew his fear was fighting desperately to overcome the growing desire to love once again. If only there was some way she could shift the balance of power, tip the scales in the direction of love.

With a sigh she crossed the kitchen and picked up the telephone. The first thing she needed to do was reassure Rose that Nanny was okay. Besides, there was really nothing she could do as far as Cliff was concerned. She'd just have to wait and bide her time until he realized he was ready to take a chance again.

By the time she finished her phone call to Rose, she was aware that the water in the shower had stopped running. Spying the coffeemaker on top of the counter, she decided to make a short pot. She was certain that Cliff, after being up all night, could use a cup, and she, too, felt a sudden craving for real caffeine. After searching several cabinets unsuccessfully for a can of coffee and filters, she finally gave up. "Hey, Cliff, where do you hide your coffee?" She waited a moment but there was no answer.

"Hey, Cliff?" She left the kitchen and walked across the living-room floor, pausing outside the bathroom door. She raised her hand to knock, then jumped as the door flew open and he emerged, practically running her over as he left the bathroom.

"Oh, sorry, I didn't know you were out here." He shifted awkwardly from foot to foot.

All thoughts of coffee fled her mind as she stared at him. His dark hair was towel-tousled and damp, giving him a vulnerable boyish appeal. However, as her gaze traveled down the length of him she found his appeal decidedly unboyish . . . totally male.

He was naked except for the towel that rode low around his slender hips. His broad chest was sprinkled with just the right amount of curly dark hairs, forming a sort of valentine pattern, the bottom of which disappeared invitingly into the top of the towel. His legs were shapely with sinewy muscles. Still, it wasn't the overwhelming masculinity of his physique that held her attention. It was his smooth, whisker-less jawline.

"You shaved," she said wondrously, reaching up and laying her palm against the smoothness of his cheek.

"Yeah." He smiled at her crookedly. "I figured I better look civilized if I'm going to take you out to lunch."

Edie was suddenly overwhelmed with the desire to be close to him again, intimate with him one more time. The roller-coaster ride of the past couple hours, combined with a heady desire, made her realize that she wanted nothing more than to crawl into his arms and make love with him. "I don't want to go out for lunch," she murmured, knowing exactly what she did want. Her hand left his cheek and moved down the line of his jaw, down his neck, to tangle in the hair that decorated his chest. "I want to stay right here, with you. I want to make love with you again."

"Edie, you don't know what you're saying," he said with a harsh breath, taking her hand away from his chest. "You've had an emotional shock, and you're confused and upset."

"I know exactly what I'm saying," she whispered, reaching up to unweave her hair from the braid that bound it. She shook her head, the dark richness of her hair spilling down over her shoulders. She heard his ragged intake of breath as her hands moved to the bottom of her sweater.

"Edie, stop it right now. This isn't right."

"Why not?" She looked at him defiantly. "I want you, Cliff. And I know you want me, too. Why not repeat what felt so good, so right the other night?" In one swift movement she pulled the sweater over her head and dropped it to the floor, standing before him proudly in a beige silk bra.

"Edie, listen to me." He grabbed her shoulders, then quickly released her as if the feel of her warm, silken skin stung him. "I warned you before. It shouldn't have happened before. I don't have anything to give to you. Nothing except a fleeting moment in time. I won't, I can't make promises of forever, or even tomorrow." His eyes were narrowed and dark with strain and his voice was filled with a gritty intensity.

"I don't want any promises. I just want you, here and now."

With a strangled cry he pulled her to him, his lips claiming hers with a fiery burst that stole her breath away. His hands tangled themselves in her hair as his mouth plundered the depths of hers.

She pressed her body against his, moaning as her breasts made contact with his bare chest, the thin, wispy bra doing little to detract from the pleasurable contact. Her arms wrapped around him, reading his back like a sightless person reading braille, memorizing every bump, muscle and tendon.

He tore his lips from hers, his breathing ragged and harsh in her ear. "Edie...you have to tell me now. Are you absolutely certain? You understand, no strings, no promises, just this single moment." His eyes glittered dangerously.

She smiled up at him, her eyes languorous with her love for him. "I've never been more certain of anything in my whole life."

She took his hand in hers and led him into the bedroom. Once there, she gracefully shed her jeans and lay down on the bed, her body covered with the wispy bra and pair of lacy underpanties. Her eyes beckoned him to join her.

As she lay there looking at him, seeing the flames of passion consuming the darkness of his eyes, his arousal obvious even with the towel as a barrier, she was filled with the rightness of it. They were merely pawns, fulfilling the destiny intended for them.

He hesitated at the foot of the bed, his gaze greedily devouring her. His eyes warmed her, causing a flush to steal over her from head to toe. Sunshine poured through the window, warming her as intimately as his gaze, but she wanted more. She didn't want the warmth from his eyes, she wanted the flames of his touch, the fire of his possession.

"Cliff..." His name was a whisper on her lips but it was the stimulant he needed to break the stillness that had possessed him as he drank in the loveliness of her. In three swift strides he had joined her on the bed, his weight crushing down on her from breast to feet.

"Oh, Edie." His mouth recaptured hers in an urgent kiss, his tongue making love to hers. He shifted his weight to one side, a hand caressing across her collarbones, down to her bra, where his hand toyed with the lace that trimmed it. Her body writhed against his, already impatient to be rid of the last remaining barriers of clothing between them. She moaned as his hand continued to tease around the edges of her bra. She started to reach behind her to unclasp it, but he stopped her.

"Slowly... I want to take it slowly and savor every second," he breathed against her mouth, his breath hot and sweet. His words caused a shiver of delight to sweep over her, but it was nothing compared to the shudders of desire that raced through her as his mouth moved down and kissed the tip of her breast through the delicate material. The heat of his breath and the wetness of the kiss caused her to gasp breathlessly.

His hand left the edge of the bra, moving slowly across her flat stomach, his fingers moving just under the elastic of her panties. They caressed her, back and forth across her lower abdomen, never quite reaching where she needed him most. He continued to fondle her, hands sliding teasingly close, then away, making her fill with an agony of frustrated desire and un-abandoned delight. His lips followed the taunting trail of his hands, driving her exquisitely, mindlessly out of her head with passion. She'd never known there were so many erogenous places on her body, where a single touch of a hand or a flick of a tongue could drive her crazy with want—the back of her knees, the inside of her thigh, beneath her first rib. She knew what he was doing, teasing and tormenting her, driving her to the point where their consummation would be explosive. And she wanted to give to him as he was giving to her. She wanted to make this joining as wondrous for him as it was for her. She rolled over on top of him, her legs straddling his.

"What...what are you doing?" he groaned, his eyes glittering with raw emotion.

"Turnabout is fair play." She leaned down and kissed him, at the same time raising up enough to re-move the towel that had been an annoying encum-brance between them.

She slowly removed her lips from his, moving them down his jaw, across his neck and settling on one of his flat male nipples. The taste of him was elixir to her soul, feeding the already flaming blaze of desire like lighter fluid on a fire. She was drunk on the feel of his flesh, the scent of his skin.

Cliff shut his eyes, trying to still the shudders that jerked his body as her tongue flicked and teased. She raised her head and he sighed with a mixture of relief and regret. The sensation of her tongue against his skin was instantly replaced by a new, different sensation. The tips of her silky hair hanging over her shoulders moved across his skin, making him groan in almost painful pleasure. Her hair danced across him, caressing the hard planes of his stomach, the turgid hardness of his groin. With an anguished moan he rolled over on top of her, his hands fumbling to unclasp her bra.

She moaned as his hands fondled the fullness of her breasts. She knew what he wanted, because she wanted the same thing. No more teasing, no more tormenting. She wanted to feel his flesh against hers. She wanted . . . no, needed to have him inside her.

She aided him, kicking off her panties, crying out as he moved his weight on top of her once again. For a moment their gazes met and held, speaking the language of lovers, transmitting subliminal messages that only their souls could hear, then with a deep surge of his body he entered her.

For a moment he didn't move and she looked up at him. His face was strained, the tendons of his neck corded with tension.

She realized he was fighting for control, warning her that he had none. He didn't realize that she was filled with him, that if he were to stop right now, she would be completely satisfied.

Her nails slowly raked down his back as she moved her hips against his. "It's all right," she murmured, urging him again with the thrust of her hips.

What little control he had maintained broke. His body drove forward against hers, making her cry out unintelligibly against his chest. They fell into a frenzied rhythm, as if they were longtime lovers accustomed to the other's needs. There was no tentativeness, no hesitancy. They fit together as if they had been making love for years.

Edie felt her muscles contracting as she climbed higher and higher toward the pinnacle of pleasure. She grasped him closer and closer, wanting to swallow him up inside her, keep him there for an eternity. As she reached her peak she gasped, at the same time feeling his body go rigid as he reached his own release. They spiraled downward together, gasping and clutching each other, wordless in the wonder.

He lay heavy on her for a moment, then moved slightly, so he was right next to her. As she gazed at him, loving him with her eyes, joy surged through her, a happiness so intense it brought the sparkle of tears to her eyes.

His eyes were closed, his thick lashes casting shadows onto his cheeks. She marveled at the beauty of his face, so naked and exposed without the cover of whiskers. She searched his face hungrily. She noticed a small mole by the side of his mouth, a treasure that had been hidden by his growth of beard. Each and every feature was studied and tucked away in her mind, to be remembered and savored later. She also noticed how tired he looked, with lines of fatigue creasing his brow, and she remembered how long it had been since he had slept.

She blushed as she remembered how forward she had been with him, taking the initiative and telling him exactly what she wanted. She had never done that before and it suddenly was important that he know that. "Cliff, I hope you don't think I make a habit of...uh...doing this."

He cracked an eyelid and looked at her. "I know that, Edie," he said softly, then closed his eyes once again.

"Well, I just want you to know that I don't make love to every policeman that comes to my door."

She was satisfied when a small smile touched his lips. She gently disengaged herself from him and started to get up, knowing he needed to sleep.

"What are you doing?"

She smiled down at him, realizing he was already about half-asleep. "I'm going to shower, then call a taxi to take me home."

"Don't be silly, I'll take you home." His eyes remained closed.

She leaned over and kissed each of his eyelids. "Don't you be silly. You stay right here and sleep. I'll see you tonight at the apartment."

Once she had disappeared into the bathroom and he heard the water running in the shower, Cliff rolled over on his back and threw an arm across his eyes.

Sleep was the farthest thing from his mind. Instead, his thoughts were playing and replaying over what had just happened between them. Oh, God, he hadn't wanted this to happen again. It had been bad enough when it had happened the first time.

He had fought against this from the first moment he had walked into her apartment. He hadn't wanted to hear the whisper of her warm sighs and sweet moans. He hadn't wanted to know the secrets of her body, the swells and curves, the softness and fire. Intimacy made distance so difficult, and the thing he needed most now was distance.

He didn't want a relationship with Edie. Love promised hope, needed commitment. Love couldn't flourish without the promise of a future. He knew she cared about him. It had been there in her eyes, in her every touch as they had made love. And her love was so seductive. But what she didn't realize was that she was in love with a shell of a man. He'd rather be emotionally dead than risk being hurt again.

Oh, it would be easy to fall into what Edie offered—caring, laughter, love. But he was afraid. Hope could be so cruel, and he couldn't go through it all again, the loving, then the losing.

He tensed as he heard the water in the shower stop running, then the sound of her humming joyously. As she came out of the bathroom he didn't move. He could hear the sounds of her dressing and he remained completely motionless. He continued to pretend to sleep as she leaned over and kissed him softly on the cheek. It wasn't until he heard the door to his apartment close, signaling that she was gone, that he expelled a ragged breath.

He had to stop this now, before it went any further. He knew it was going to hurt her, but it would only get worse if he allowed their relationship to continue. He had reached out once for love and been badly burned. He would be a fool to tempt fate twice. He knew he was right to retreat, yet he couldn't control the bleak, vast emptiness that filled him as he contemplated his life without her. Then, for the first time in years, Cliff wept.

Eight

"Edie told me to let you in when you arrived," Rose explained, fumbling through the numerous keys on the large key ring, searching for the one that would open Edie's apartment door. "Dear girl, she slept for a little while this afternoon, then hurried right back to the hospital." She tried unsuccessfully to insert another key. "Poor Nanny, every time I think about seeing her lying there at the foot of the stairs...so still..." She paused to wipe a grief-plumped tear from her face. "Thank God Edie has you, Mr. Marchelli. She's going to need you what with Nanny in the hospital and all."

Cliff tightened his grip on the duffel bag handles, not wanting to hear that Edie needed him. He sighed with relief as Rose finally found the right key and the door clicked open.

"There you are. Edie told me to tell you she'll be home later. She wanted to stay at the hospital until Nanny was asleep for the night."

Cliff thanked her, then gratefully slipped into the silence of the Turner apartment. The first thing he saw was the bowl of strawberries sitting in the middle of the table, washed and stemmed, ready to be popped into his mouth. With all the worry about Nanny, Edie had still remembered to fix him a bowl of the strawberries. For some reason the thought depressed him.

It had been a strange afternoon, holding both the dizzying heights of joy and the depths of despair.

At first his tears had frightened him. He hadn't been sure where they came from or exactly what caused them. Then he'd suddenly realized they were the result of years of emotion bottled up tightly inside. Once they had begun to fall he could no more stop them than he could stop the spray of liquid from an uncorked, shaken bottle of champagne.

Initially his tears had been for Catherine. The grief he'd never acknowledged had exploded out of him in waves, leaving him weak and spent. Then he had cried for himself, for the dreams that had been stolen from him, making him afraid to ever dream again. Then he had slept.

When he'd awakened, he'd immediately recognized that something was different. His tears had been cathartic, washing away the bitter seeds of despair that had lain fertile but dormant for the past two years. He'd felt cleansed, lighter, as if an enormous weight had been lifted from his shoulders. He hadn't realized what a heavy poundage his grief had been until it had been dispelled.

Still, he was steadfast in his resolve to end the relationship with Edie. His tears could not banish the fact that he would never risk falling in love and being hurt. As he looked at the bowl of strawberries and felt depression settle around him, he knew what was happening. He was going into a new grieving process, bereaving the loss of Edie and the future emptiness of his life.

He settled into his seat at the window, wondering why it was that doing the right thing was always so painful.

It had been such a long night, Edie thought as she got out of her car and stepped into the predawn. Her footsteps grew quicker as she sprinted up the flight of stairs that led to her apartment. Cliff was there, and at the moment she needed him desperately.

She unlocked her door and walked in, seeing him standing at the window. Without hesitation she moved to him and wrapped her arms around his neck, burrowing her face in his broad chest.

"Oh, Cliff, hold me," she murmured, tightening her grip around him. She felt his momentary hesitation, then his arms went tightly around her and she closed her eyes. For a long moment they stood there, with her in his arms breathing in his scent, pressing her body into the now-familiar planes of his body.

"Did—did something happen? Did Nanny take a turn for the worse?" His deep voice made his chest vibrate beneath her cheek.

She sighed and reluctantly pulled herself a few inches away from him. "No, physically she's fine." She moved out of his arms and sat on the sofa. Cliff moved away from the window and sat next to her. "Oh, Cliff, she didn't know me." Tears spilled soundlessly and she wiped at them impatiently. "I know I'm being ridiculous. There have been lots of times in the past when she didn't know exactly who I was, but this time was different." She sighed tremulously as Cliff took her hand in his, silently encouraging her to continue. "Always before, even when she didn't recognize me as her granddaughter, Edie, she knew me as somebody who cared for her, somebody she could trust. But last night she didn't know me at all, and she seemed so frightened." Suddenly the emotion she had been holding in since the moment she had walked up the sidewalk and had seen the ambulance pulling away escaped. Tears chased each other down her face in a frenzied game of tag, and with a sob she reached again for Cliff.

"Let it all out," he crooned, feeling the sobs that shook her body as he stroked her hair and held her close against his chest. He knew the tears would have a cleansing relief as they had for him earlier in the day.

And she did let it all out. She sobbed until there were no more tears left, just convulsive dry heaves that racked her body and made her throat scratchy and her head pound.

She finally pulled away from him with a small, self-conscious laugh. "I'm sorry, I feel so ridiculous and I've absolutely soaked your shirt."

"You shouldn't feel ridiculous and my shirt will dry."

She looked at him gratefully, then rubbed her forehead where it throbbed with pain.

"Headache?"

She nodded.

He stood and disappeared into the kitchen, returning to the sofa with a glass of water. "Drink this. Then what you really need is some sleep." He watched as she drank the water like an obedient child, then he held out his hand to her. "Come on, I'll tuck you in, then I'll get out of here so you can get some undisturbed sleep."

She allowed him to help her up and lead her into her bedroom. Yes, what she needed was some rest. Not only did her head ache, but her eyes felt gritty and burned with the combination of tears and sheer exhaustion.

As he turned down the covers on the bed, she went into the bathroom and changed into her caftan.

"Okay, in you go," Cliff said as she crawled beneath the blanket of the small bed. He pulled the sheet up around her neck and sat on the edge of the bed. "You know, Nanny was probably confused because she'd been sedated and the surroundings were unfamiliar. I'm sure things will be better the next time you see her."

She smiled, her eyes heavy with the need for sleep. "I'm sure you're right." He started to pull his hand away, stopping as she spoke his name. "Will you stay with me for a few minutes, just until I fall asleep?"

He hesitated. There was no seduction in her eyes, no promise of invitation, only the need of one human being to be comforted by the presence of another. Yet he was afraid. He couldn't get any more deeply involved with her.

"Please?" Her eyes silently begged him.

He relented. "All right."

She scooted over, making room for him to stretch out beside her on the narrow bed. "Just lie here with me for a little while and hold me," she murmured.

What harm could there be in granting this request? he asked himself as he lay down beside her. She was shaken by Nanny's condition and she wanted to be comforted. Surely he could grant her this. He gathered her into his arms. It was the least he could do for her before he walked out of her life for good. He'd leave just as soon as she fell asleep.

He closed his eyes, enjoying the feel of her soft breath warming his neck. *How can something that feels so right be so wrong?* he wondered just before he fell into a deep, dreamless sleep.

Edie awoke slowly, finding herself lying on her side, pressed tightly against his body. Her head rested in the curve of his shoulder, her thigh caught between his legs.

She moved her head slightly so she could look up at his face, marvel at the love she felt for him. He was asleep, his deep, rhythmic breathing moving his chest against hers. Yes, she loved this man. She'd known him such an incredibly short time, yet she was sure of the emotion that beat in her heart.

She had thought her commitment to taking care of Nanny filled her life, but she suddenly saw all the empty corners her existence had contained before he entered her world.

And he cared for her, too. She knew it as surely as she knew the sun would rise in the mornings and the winter followed the fall. She knew it by the look in his eyes, the touch of his hand, the way he had held her so gently when she needed to cry.

She stroked his face tenderly, tracing over the contours of his brow, his cheek, his lips. It was such a strong face, holding lines that were testimony of life. He stirred, tightening his arms around her, but didn't awaken.

She pressed her lips against the smooth skin of his neck, her hands beginning to dance across his chest, down the flat planes of his stomach, lingering hesitantly at the buckle of his belt. Should she wake him up? He seemed to be sleeping so peacefully. She smiled in anticipation, her hands fumbling to unfasten his jeans. Why not awaken him? There were so many more interesting things to do than sleep.

Cliff was plunged from sleep to consciousness to full-blown desire in the space of seconds, with no time to mentally make the transition. Consciousness came with a gasp of surprise as he felt her hands dipping beneath the belt of his jeans, exploring the only part of his anatomy that seemed to be completely awake.

The resolve to never make love with her again was trapped someplace deep within him as he realized she

was naked and his hands made contact with her warm
flesh. He groaned as she leaned over him, tugging at
his pants. The afternoon sunlight streamed into the
bedroom window, dancing on her skin, giving it a
burnished golden glow.

As her lips replaced her hands on him, the last vestige of denial fled his mind. She was a honey-hued
witch who had taken possession of him, body, mind
and soul. His shirt quickly followed the direction of
his jeans and her caftan, landing in a pile on the floor.
The small bed beneath them creaked and groaned as
they became all flesh and tangled sheets and urgent
sighs.

They moved against each other in unabandoned
delight, rediscovering the same joy they had found
together the day before. No words were spoken. None
were needed. Their bodies said everything that needed
to be said. Then he was in her, filling her, taking her
with him on a journey to the sky. And as they reached
it she clung to him, whispering his name over and over
again reverently like a prayer.

"I guess I'm going to have to invest in a double
bed," she said with a grin, stroking his hair as he lay
across her chest.

Cliff tensed at her words, reality intruding and
making him realize the magnitude of what he had
done. This should never have happened again. It was
only going to make everything more difficult. Oh,
God, he had to be strong. He had to cut himself out of
her life now, before irreparable harm was done to her.

"Edie." He rolled away from her and right off the side of the bed. He hit the floor with a thud and her giggles filled the room.

She leaned over the side of the bed, looking more like a mischievous imp than the woman who had just driven him insane with passion. He knew in that instant that he couldn't tell her, at least not at the moment. The mood was all wrong. He couldn't tell her now, not with his skin still smelling of hers, the taste of her still in his mouth. He couldn't tell her there was no hope for them with their bodies still slick with the sheen from their lovemaking, her eyes still glowing in the aftermath of love.

"What time is it?" he asked, grabbing his jeans from the floor.

"Almost five o'clock. We were asleep for a long time." She stretched languidly, watching him as he dressed. It was pleasant, lying back and watching him as he pulled his jeans up over his slender hips and pulled the shirt on to cover his broad shoulders. She'd never known that watching a man dress could be so stimulating.

"I've got to go. I've got to check in at that station." He finished buttoning his shirt.

"Give me a kiss before you go," she demanded with a bewitching smile.

"Edie, I'm going to be late," he protested, desperation making his stomach start to burn. He needed to get out of here, get some distance from her. She overwhelmed him—the look in her eyes, the satin softness of her skin.

"Cliff Marchelli, surely you can take one minute and give me a kiss," she exclaimed, stung by his brusque answer.

Cliff, seeing the stricken look on her face, leaned over, aiming for her cheek. But she turned her face and captured his lips with hers. He didn't fight the kiss; instead he savored it. He memorized the sweetness of her mouth, the scent of her hair, the erotic feel of her tongue against his. He wanted to remember everything he could about the kiss because he knew it was a kiss of goodbye.

After he left, Edie got out of bed and took a long, hot shower. As she stood beneath the spray of water, her mind played and replayed the past two days with Cliff. It was funny—she had never before realized how incomplete she had been, not until she'd felt the completeness of her and Cliff together. She knew she should be cautious, that he had made no promises, but it was hard to be cautious when in love.

After showering she donned a cinnamon-colored sweater dress that she knew flattered her figure and brought out the auburn highlights of her hair. She carefully applied her makeup and brushed her hair until it gleamed. She was only going to the hospital, but she felt so happy, so beautiful inside, she wanted that showing on the outside.

As she left her apartment, on impulse she knocked on Rose's door.

"Ah, Edie, love, come on in." Rose admitted her into the apartment. "Cup of coffee?" she asked, gesturing to one of the chairs at the table.

"Okay," Edie agreed, sitting down. "Where's Tony?" she asked, noticing there was no sign of Rose's son.

"He left this morning, went back home."

Edie nodded. "I was on my way to the hospital and realized I hadn't thanked you for putting away all the stuff I got at the city market the other day."

"Ah, it was the least I could do." Rose poured them each a cup of coffee, then joined Edie at the table. She looked at Edie for a long moment, her gaze openly speculative. "You look awfully nice to be going to the hospital. In fact, you're positively glowing."

"I just felt like getting dressed up."

"This glow on your face, it wouldn't have anything to do with a certain Italian man who has cute buns, would it?"

"It might." Edie smiled mysteriously, but she couldn't sustain the noncommittal answer. She was too happy and she wanted to share her happiness with everyone around her. In fact, she wanted to shout from the top of the highest building that she was in love with Cliff Marchelli. "Oh, Rose, he's so wonderful, and he makes me feel so wonderful."

Rose's dark eyes twinkled brightly. "It sounds like love."

"It feels like love, and I think he feels the same way." Edie paused, sipping her coffee, then continued thoughtfully. "But it's hard to tell what he feels. He keeps all his emotions closely guarded. He hasn't exactly told me that he loves me, at least not verbally, but I know he does."

Rose nodded. "Men are about as anxious to tell a woman they love them as a kid is excited to get a tetanus shot."

"Yes, but Cliff has had some tragedy in his past and I think it's made him afraid to love anyone again."

"Oh, pooh, every man is afraid to make a commitment. Johnny and I dated for a year without him telling me he loved me or making a commitment. I finally told him to fish or cut bait." A nostalgic smile swept across Rose's face. "I told him if he wasn't ready to commit to me, then there was a very handsome meat cutter who had been making eyes at me. Johnny bought me an engagement ring the very next night."

"Was there a handsome meat cutter making eyes at you?" Edie asked curiously.

"Sure there was." Rose's smile widened. "Of course, I didn't bother to tell Johnny that the meat cutter was sixty years old, married and had grandchildren."

Edie laughed appreciatively. She finished her coffee, then stood. "I'd better get over to the hospital. I'm anxious to see how Nanny is doing."

Rose got up and walked with her to the door. "Give Nanny my love. Tell her I'm thinking about her."

"I will."

"And Edie, about this Cliff. If you love him, truly love him and you believe he feels the same way, don't let anything stand in your way. Love is so hard to come by, and I can tell by the glow on your face that you've found it with this man. If you love him, go after him. Chase him until he catches you."

Edie laughed and gave the short, broad woman an affectionate hug. "Thanks for the advice."

"Oh, I'm always good at giving advice." Rose laughed. "Just ask Anthony's fiancée. She'll tell you all about my free advice."

"That reminds me, how are the wedding plans coming along?"

Rose shrugged. "What do I know? I'm just the mother of the groom."

"I'm sure everything will turn out just fine." Edie gave her another hug, then said goodbye, left the apartment and headed for her car.

As she drove toward the hospital she mulled over the conversation she'd had with Rose. Who would have thought that when she opened her apartment door to admit one of Kansas City's finest, she had also been admitting love into her home and heart? Who would have believed that a hard-boiled, cynical cop with ulcers could have managed to bring love into her life? She, Cliff and Nanny... in this particular case three wasn't a crowd, three was a family.

"Slow down, girl," she whispered to herself as she pulled the car into the hospital parking lot. She, more than anyone, knew Cliff's reticence in getting involved in a relationship.

One day at a time, that was the way she would have to go with Cliff. One day after another, golden days of making love and laughter together, building a bond that would make Cliff believe in the future. He was like a young boy, diving off the high dive for the very first time. Each day he'd climb one rung higher and be less frightened. Then suddenly one day he would be up on the top of the platform and jump over the edge, and his fear would only be a distant memory. Each day she saw Cliff taking another step, getting closer and closer to her, and one of these days his fear would be all gone.

Her positive thoughts put an energetic spring in her step as she walked into the hospital and to room 202.

"I'm going to tan your hide if you don't stop pricking me with those needles and keeping me up all hours of the night. I've never heard of waking a body up to give her a pill to go to sleep."

The sound of Nanny's strident voice made Edie move quickly to the room, where she found Dr. Stafford trying to placate the irritable woman.

"Edie." The doctor looked up as she entered the room, gazing at her as if she were his personal savior.

"Dr. Stafford." Edie smiled at the doctor. "Nanny, are you giving the doctor a hard time?" she asked lightly.

"Hrrumph. They're making me eat runny food and sticking my arm full of needles and won't let me get up out of this bed and you think I'm giving *him* a hard time?" Nanny glared up at Dr. Stafford.

"Could I speak with you for a few moments out in the hall?" he asked Edie. She nodded and followed him out into the hallway. "Whew, she can be quite strong willed."

Edie laughed. "You don't have to be diplomatic with me, Dr. Stafford. I know she can be a real handful when she gets in one of her moods."

"She dumped her breakfast tray this morning, said she wanted Bessie's boy to bring her tacos."

Edie smiled at this, filing it away to share with Cliff later. "I'm sorry if she's giving you and the nurses a hard time."

"It's not myself or the nurses I'm concerned about, it's your grandmother." Dr. Stafford looked at Edie seriously.

"You haven't found anything else wrong, have you? You did say the collarbone break was the only real problem from the fall."

"No, it's nothing like that," he hurriedly assured her. "However, I am concerned about the fact that she seems to be so unsettled about being here. As you know, she hardly slept at all last night, and she hasn't had any sleep so far today. Her body can't heal as quickly if she can't rest. That's what I was doing in there a few minutes ago, trying to get her to take a mild sleeping tablet. It would help alleviate some of her anxiety and help her get some much-needed rest."

"Do you have the tablet?"

Dr. Stafford nodded and dropped the little pill into Edie's palm.

"I'll see that she takes it," Edie said.

"Edie, have you thought about what arrangements you're going to make for your grandmother when I release her from here?"

Edie sighed, a frown creasing her brow. "Yes, I've thought and thought, but I still haven't come up with what I consider a viable solution. I know I can no longer take care of Nanny alone. She requires more supervision than any one person can give. But I can't find it in my heart to think that a nursing home is a reasonable alternative."

"Actually, I don't think a nursing home is the answer. Your grandmother is still in fairly good health other than her Alzheimer's disease. Of course, her long-term prognosis is not good. Eventually she'll have to be fed, with all her basic needs attended to— *then* is the time to consider a nursing home. Have you thought about paying a private nurse to come in and care for her a few hours each day?"

"Actually, I hadn't thought about it, but that does seem to be a reasonable solution. Is it necessary that it be a nurse?"

Dr. Stafford shook his head. "In essence, Edie, what you need is a baby-sitter. Somebody who can watch her when you can't to see that she doesn't get herself into any problems."

"I'll check into getting somebody immediately," she replied, relieved that at least a solution seemed to be at hand. "When do you think she can come home?"

"I'd like to keep her for at least another week, make sure that collarbone is healing properly and there are no other complications."

Edie nodded. "Thank you for your time, Dr. Stafford. And I'll see to it that Nanny gets this pill." She shook the doctor's hand, then went into the hospital room.

"Well, I suppose he filled your head all full of lies," Nanny said as Edie reentered the room.

"Actually, he told me he was very concerned about you because you haven't been sleeping." Edie pulled a chair up to the side of the bed.

"I don't want to sleep. If I go to sleep, who knows where I'll wake up. Last time I fell asleep, I ended up here. I don't like it here. I want to go home."

"Nanny, you need to sleep. Now, I want you to take this pill. It will make you feel better."

"No." Nanny clamped her lips tightly together, looking like a child about to be given a dose of castor oil.

Edie stroked Nanny's hand soothingly. "Remember when I was little and I'd be sick and I didn't want to take the medicine that would make me feel better? You'd sit next to my bed, just like I'm doing right now. You'd hold out the little pill and you'd say, 'Edie, I know this looks like a silly little pill, but actually it's much more than that. This little pill holds fifty leprechauns, special leprechauns that are armed to fight the bad stuff in your body.' You remember that?"

Nanny shook her head, the story not sparking an ounce of remembrance. "Is it true? Are there leprechauns?"

"That's what you always told me. And you'd say that if I took the pill you'd tell me wonderful stories that would keep a happy smile on my face while the pill was doing its magic on the inside of my body."

Nanny was silent for a long moment. "If I take that pill, will you tell me wonderful stories?"

Edie nodded, sighing with relief as Nanny took the tablet from her, popped it into her mouth and swallowed audibly.

"Now, tell me a story," Nanny demanded.

* * *

Cliff walked slowly down the hospital corridor, unsure exactly what he was doing there. He supposed it had to do with the fact that he wanted to see Nanny one more time, tell her goodbye. He'd already mentally said his goodbye to Edie.

He'd brought a bag of tacos with him. It was funny, really. Nanny didn't know who he was. She went from thinking him a Peeping Tom pervert to Bessie's son, but she had made an indelible mark on his heart. He admired her dignity, enjoyed her spunkiness, sensed her caring heart—all traits that had been passed to her granddaughter. It was through Edie and Nanny's caring that Cliff had finally been able to face his grief over Catherine, face it and be rid of it. He supposed this final visit was a sort of thank-you to Nanny, for being a part of his healing process.

He paused just outside Nanny's room, hearing the familiar tones of Edie's voice. Damn, he hadn't wanted to run into her. He wasn't ready to face her yet. He'd hoped she would still be at home.

He shifted from foot to foot, unsure what to do. As he stood there indecisively, Edie's words drifted out to him.

"And the three of us will live in a big house and you'll have your very own room."

"With violets on the wallpaper," Nanny said, her voice sluggish with sleep. "I love violets, don't you?"

"Yes, with violets on the wallpaper," Edie agreed. "And every Sunday I'll cook us platters of tacos. Then we'll all sit on the back porch while Cliff mows the lawn."

"And what will I be doing?" Nanny asked.

"You'll be playing with your great-grandchildren."

"Oh, that's so nice. You tell good stories," Nanny said softly.

Cliff's heart lurched in his chest at the fantasies Edie spun. A house, a lawn, children...he had to stop her. He had to make her understand. He'd promised nothing. She had said she understood that he couldn't give her anything but a single moment of his passion.

He turned and ran out of the hospital. Tonight...tonight he had to tell her there was no future, that it had all been a mistake. Oh, God, he hated the hurt he knew he was going to inflict on her, but it was a necessary hurt, like lancing a boil. He had grieved Catherine's loss; he'd healed that particular pain. But his loss of faith, his long-lost belief that love conquers all—that could never be healed. He'd lost his innocence, and the sad part was he had a feeling that because of him, Edie was going to lose hers, as well.

Edie knew something had happened the minute she drove down the street in front of the apartment. Police cars were everywhere and neighbors who hadn't been seen out in months were standing in front of their homes, wrapped in various degrees of nightclothes.

She parked her car and hurried around to the front of the building, where Rose and several of the other tenants were chattering with excitement.

"Oh, Edie, love. You missed all the excitement." Rose greeted her, her plump face red with excitement, her body covered in a bright purple muumuu.

"What happened?" Edie asked, but she knew. Cliff's big bust had occurred.

"It was just a few minutes past ten o'clock when all of a sudden a million police cars came roaring up to the warehouse." Rose pointed across the street, where several policemen were coming out of the building.

"There wasn't a million police cars," Bernie Westfall, the seventy-year-old man who lived on the third floor, interjected. Edie tried to hide a smile. He wore a pair of pajamas with black patent dress shoes and a suit jacket thrown over his shoulders. The swirling red police lights reflected on the shiny baldness of his head. "There were six. I counted them, there were six," he explained.

"Well, it looked like a million," Rose continued, shooting a glare at Bernie. "They had their lights flashing and their sirens screaming. They screeched to a stop and all the policemen jumped out of their cars with their guns ready."

"They didn't have their guns out. I saw, I was watching the whole thing and they didn't have their guns out," Bernie protested.

Rose huffed with exasperation. "Anyway, they got on a loudspeaker and told the men in the warehouse to put their hands up and come out."

"It's called a bullhorn, not a loudspeaker," Bernie explained.

"Do you want to tell this story?" Rose asked, putting her hands on her ample hips and glaring at him.

Bernie shrugged. "No, go ahead. You're doing fine."

Edie stifled a giggle as Rose continued. "Anyway, the police arrested a bunch of men and took away a whole van full of drugs." Rose shot a smug look at Bernie, as if pleased that she had been able to finish the story her way.

"Sounds really exciting," Edie said, anxious to get upstairs to Cliff. He would be happy that everything had gone so well. They could celebrate—she had a bottle of champagne someplace. Champagne, candlelight and love...it was going to be a memorable night.

Telling her friends goodbye, she raced up the stairway and burst into her apartment. He was gone. The camera equipment, the binoculars, everything was gone, as if he had only been a figment of her imagination.

"Of course he's gone," she chided herself. "He's a cop, and he was just part of a major drug bust." She sat on the sofa, let down even though her mind rationalized his absence. Of course he would have to go straight down to the station and take care of all kinds of details. He couldn't hang around here and share in a celebration. He'd still have lots of work to do. We'll celebrate tomorrow, she thought, rising from the sofa and going to the kitchen cabinets. It took her several minutes of hunting before she finally located the dusty bottle of champagne. She couldn't even remember when she had bought it. She blew the dust off and stuck it in the refrigerator to chill.

There was a part of her that was disappointed that the bust had really happened. Cliff would no longer have a reason to be here in her apartment. He wouldn't be there at the window when she went to bed at night. *But that's all right,* she consoled herself. *Now when I go to bed, instead of being at my window he'll be in bed beside me.* The end of his assignment did not mean the end of their relationship. What they had begun building together in the past week could not be easily dismissed just because he would no longer be in her apartment in an official capacity.

He'll be here tomorrow, she assured herself. *He'll come over and we'll celebrate his success with the bust.* Oh, yes, this was just the beginning for them. She hugged herself with happiness.

Nine

"**I** don't believe it." Walt stared at Cliff in disbelief. "You look almost human."

Cliff flushed, running a hand over his newly cut hair. "Yeah, well, I figured it was about time."

Walt nodded his approval. "By the way, the police commissioner sends his congratulations on a job well done. That bust the other night took two major drug dealers off the streets. They'll be making their deals from now on from a jail cell in Leavenworth." Walt smiled in satisfaction. "I must say, thanks to those arrests the record of my final year as police chief will look quite impressive."

"Good. While you're feeling so expansive, I'd like to make a request."

"Name it."

"I'd like some time off."

Walt looked at him in surprise. "No problem. You know you have plenty of time accrued. You haven't had a vacation since your wife...uh...for the past couple of years."

Cliff smiled to ease the older man's discomfort. "You can say it. It's all right. I haven't had any time off since Catherine divorced me." He knew how his co-workers had tiptoed around the topic of his divorce for the past two years because of his own inability to accept the blow fate had dealt to him. "I'd like to take two weeks, starting today," Cliff explained.

"You've got it," Walt agreed, eyeing Cliff speculatively. "Is everything all right?"

"Everything is fine. I'm going to take a drive to St. Louis and visit with my mother and her husband for a few days."

"Good, good. It's always nice to visit family." Walt nodded, obviously pleased with Cliff's decision.

Cliff stood. "Then I'll be back in two weeks." He pulled a folded piece of paper out of his back pocket and handed it across the desk to Walt. "This is the address and phone number at my mother's place. Just in case something comes up and you need me for anything."

Walt stood and extended his hand to Cliff, who shook it warmly. "Enjoy your time off, Cliff. You've earned it."

"Thanks, Walt. I'll check back in when I get home."

Cliff left the police station and got into his car, heading back to his apartment. As he drove, his thoughts turned to Edie. She hadn't been far from his mind in the past three days, ever since the night of the bust. He knew he had taken the cowardly way out, leaving the apartment while she wasn't at home. But at that point things had been out of his control. The bust had gone down quickly, then he'd needed to rush down to the station and aid in the booking of the suspects. Night had turned into morning by the time he'd finished the necessary paperwork.

Each morning since then he'd awakened with thoughts of her plaguing his mind. But he knew he had to let her go. It was the right thing to do. He was right to walk away from Edie. It was right to walk away from love.

Three days and not a word. Edie really hadn't expected to see Cliff on the night of the bust. However, she had been surprised when she didn't hear from him the following day.

For the first time in her life she found herself contemplating the merits of an answering machine. She had sworn to herself long ago that she would never own one, fearing the day when machines would forever banish the warmth of a real, human voice. But in the past three days, as she divided her time between the apartment and the hospital, she found herself wondering if maybe Cliff had tried to call her while she had been out.

It was on the afternoon of the third day following the bust that she had to face the harsh reality. He hadn't called, and chances were he wasn't going to call.

She sat at the kitchen table with a cup of tea, staring out the window where he had been an unwelcome intruder and had become a welcomed guest. When he left the night of the arrests, he had rehung the plant that they had taken down, but the area looked curiously empty without his presence. Funny, it had never looked that way before. She jumped as a knock sounded on her door. It opened and Rose walked in.

"Don't get up," Rose instructed, walking over to the stove where the teakettle was still warm and helping herself to a cup of tea. "I came to see how you were getting along," she said, sitting at the table across from Edie.

"I'm getting along fine."

Rose frowned. "You look pale."

"I'm spending a lot of time at the hospital. I guess I'm just a little tired," she confessed, although she didn't go on to say that when she did finally get a chance to sleep, she tossed and turned with dreams of Cliff.

"I thought they were only keeping Nanny at the hospital for a day or two of observation. Why hasn't she come home yet?" Rose asked worriedly, stirring a liberal heaping of sugar into her herbal tea.

"They decided that as long as they had her there for her collarbone they'd do a little physical therapy on her legs, see if they can increase her circulation and mobility."

Rose nodded and sipped her tea thoughtfully. "Have you decided what you're going to do when she is released?"

Edie shook her head. "Not yet. I'm beginning to think perhaps the best thing would be a nursing home, but I haven't made a definite decision." At the moment, with thoughts of Cliff weighing heavily on her mind, the job of making a decision concerning Nanny's future seemed overwhelming.

"Edie, something else is bothering you. I can see it on your face." Rose reached over and covered Edie's hands with hers. "I haven't been able to help but notice that your young man hasn't been around for the last couple of days."

Edie smiled. She should have realized that Rose would have noticed Cliff's absence. "Rose, Cliff is a police officer for the Kansas City Police Department. He's been here on a surveillance job. He was responsible for all the excitement here the other night."

"So, that doesn't tell me why he hasn't been around here since."

Edie shrugged. "His job is finished, and so he left." She tried to keep the pain out of her voice, but as she looked at Rose's sympathetic face, she knew she had been unsuccessful.

"When you told me you loved him, that wasn't true? That was just a story so we wouldn't know he was a cop?"

How Edie wished it was just a story, that she had only pretended to love Cliff for the sake of an arrest. That would have made things so much less complicated, so much less painful. "No, that wasn't a story, that was the truth," she finally answered softly.

"So, what are you going to do now?"

Edie looked at Rose helplessly. "What can I do?"

"Fight for him," Rose answered without hesitation. "Have you told him you love him?"

Edie shook her head slowly. "No, I haven't actually said the words, but surely he knows how I feel about him." Her mind raced, replaying the intimate moments she and Cliff had shared. Surely he knew. How could he not know how she felt about him?

"Oh, honestly, Edie. Men can be such meatheads at times. If you love him and you want him to remain a part of your life, tell him. If he's important to you, fight for him." Rose got up suddenly, finished her tea and placed her cup in the sink. "I'm going to leave you now. I think you should take my advice." She grinned. "But then, I think everyone should always take my advice." With this she left Edie alone.

Edie stared into her now-empty cup, wishing she knew how to read tea leaves, and what the dregs in the bottom of her cup would tell her.

Fight for him. Rose's words reverberated in her head like the lyrics of an old song that refused to be forgotten. But shouldn't pride play some part in this? she wondered. Yet pride made such a cold bedfellow, and to sacrifice the chance of a lifetime of love for a moment's pride seemed such a foolish thing to do.

With her decision made, she got up from the table and grabbed her car keys. She was going to face him. She needed to confront him, look into his eyes as she told him of her love for him. She couldn't be so wrong, she couldn't have just imagined the love she'd seen reflected in his eyes as he held her in his arms. And if she was wrong, if he really didn't care about her, she needed to hear it from him. She needed a closure to the relationship, a definite end rather than this uncommitted silence.

She hurried out of her apartment before she had a chance to change her mind. Now that the decision had been made she was anxious to get on with it.

She concentrated on her driving, not wanting to rehearse in her mind what she was going to say to him. She wanted her words to come from her heart, not from a well-practiced speech.

When she got to his apartment she didn't hesitate, but got out of her car and strode purposefully to his door. She knocked loudly, as if the resounding noise could buoy her with courage. But as she waited for an answer, her insides trembled like a leaf shivering on a windy autumn day.

Then suddenly the door flew open and he stood before her. He wore navy cords and a pale blue dress shirt, the shirt untucked, the cuffs unbuttoned as if he had just slipped the shirt on. She had never seen him in dress clothes before, and her heart swelled in her chest as she gazed at him hungrily.

"Edie." His voice held surprise and his gaze didn't quite meet hers.

"I was just in the neighborhood and thought I'd drop by and say hello," she said lightly, fighting the small niggling anger that surged up unexpectedly as his eyes refused to meet hers. He acted like a young man who had indulged in a one-night stand, then to his horror and embarrassment had found the unwanted girl sitting on his front porch the following morning.

"Uh...come on in." He opened the door wider to allow her admittance. "Would you like something to drink, a cup of coffee or a soft drink?"

"No, thanks. I assume congratulations are in order. I saw in the newspaper that the bust was quite a success."

He nodded. "You'll be getting a letter from the police department, thanking you for your cooperation."

"I can hardly wait," she said dryly. Her gaze fell on a suitcase and duffel bag that sat on the floor near the front door. "Are you leaving the country, or going on another assignment?" she asked, pleased that her hurt wasn't reflected in her voice. He treated her so distantly, so coldly, like an acquaintance he wasn't sure he liked.

"No, just taking a trip for a couple of days."

She drew a deep breath, anger and pain mingling inside her. He was leaving town and he had not intended to call her. No goodbye, no farewell, no gee, it's been fun...nothing. For a moment the emotional storm inside her was too great to allow her speech. She turned away from him, moving woodenly across the floor. She needed to keep her back to him for a moment, until she could erase the hurt, the vulnerability from her eyes.

"Cliff."

"Edie."

They spoke at the same time, then both flushed. "Go ahead," she prompted him, sitting on the edge of the sofa and staring up at him.

For a long moment he didn't say anything. He paced back and forth several times in front of her, running his hand through his hair before he finally spoke. "Edie, I know I should have called you, but I'm not going to lie to you and tell you I was going to call before I left town." His words were slow and measured, telling of the thought going into each one. "The day after the bust, I did consider calling you, but then I decided that maybe it was best just to leave things alone, let this thing between us die of its own accord. It seemed the most painless way to handle it."

"You mean the most cowardly," she retorted painfully, then bit her bottom lip.

He looked at her fully for the first time since she had arrived. "You're right, it was cowardly. But Edie, this is no good. We're no good for each other."

"How can you even say that?" she whispered, appalled at his words. "How can you even think that it's no good when it feels so right for us to be together?"

"Yes, it feels right, and it feels good, and that's why it has got to stop right now." His eyes changed, darkening, and a muscle twitched betrayingly at the corner of his mouth. "I can't give you the things you need, the things you deserve."

"Why don't you let me decide what I need and deserve?" she returned evenly.

He shook his head. "I can't. You're young and wearing rose-tinted glasses. You think love can solve everything, but I know better. I won't take a chance on the fickleness of fate, on the uncertainty of the future."

"So instead, you'll turn your back on life, on love?" she asked softly.

"It's called the survival instinct. I've learned the fine art of self-preservation." There was a note of bold anger in his voice and his face was strained. "I gambled once and lost. I'm just not willing to gamble again."

"Cliff, I love you." She spoke humbly, as if the words themselves could erase all his fears, all his scars.

"Don't you see? That changes nothing," he returned harshly. "It just makes me sorry I let things go so far between us..."

"Cliff..." She got up off the sofa and went over to where he stood, body tense and face set as if carved in granite. "Did you love her so much, so desperately that you'll let her ruin your life?" She laid her hand gently on his arm. "A lot of people live with heartache, experience loss, but that doesn't mean you curl up and die."

He jerked away from her touch. "What the hell do you know about loss?" he asked bitterly.

Edie stared at him. The anger inside that had reared its head earlier now stood up and shouted. "How dare you. I can't believe your arrogance, that nobody has ever suffered a loss quite as profound as yours. You got a divorce, Cliff. I lost both my parents when I was a child, then I lost my grandfather and every day I lose a little bit more of Nanny. Don't talk to me about losses." Her voice trembled with her emotion.

For a long moment he said nothing. "Edie, I never meant to hurt you," he breathed, his lips forming a grimace of pain.

"Just do one thing for me," she said in a shallow whisper. "Look me in the eyes and tell me you don't care about me. Look me in the eyes and say you don't love me."

He stared at her, his eyes narrowed and black with strain. His mouth worked soundlessly and his hand swept through his hair with agitation once again. "I can't." He tore his gaze from hers, his voice an angry, despairing sound. Edie's heart swelled with happiness. So she hadn't been wrong, after all. He did care for her. His face was all harsh angles, taut with stress, and to her it was the most beautiful, beloved face in the world.

"Edie." He sighed deeply and placed his hands on her shoulders, holding her at arm's distance. "Damn it, I warned you. I told you what you could expect from me. A brief interlude, a fleeting moment in time. I never promised you anything more than that."

"Don't you understand? Fleeting moments are all any of us have. One moment built on the next until you have a lifetime." She stared at him, her frustration evident in her eyes. She shrugged his hands off her shoulders, and instead placed her palms on either side of his face. "Cliff... take a chance. Don't run away from what I have to give you. Don't punish me for what Catherine did to you."

He grabbed her wrists and pulled her hands away from his face. He hardly breathed and she could feel the wave of force in the air between them.

"You give too much," he said harshly, still gripping her wrists tightly. "You offer things that I can never reciprocate. I'm all wrong for you. I've got nothing to give you." He slackened his hold on her wrists and looked at her, raw pain emanating from his dark eyes. "I can't, Edie. I put myself on the line once, and I came up empty. I'm not willing to put myself on the line again."

She was very still, her eyes searching his face, looking for a sign of weakness, a wavering of resolve, but she saw none. "So that's it?" Her voice held a bleak, empty ring. "Just because she left you, you're just going to turn your back and walk away from me? From everything I have to give to you?"

His face hardened. "That's it." His features twisted with something painful. "Don't you understand, Edie? I'm afraid." He tore his gaze away from her, as if ashamed of this confession.

"So you're going to allow your fear to make you an emotional cripple." She tried to keep her voice steady. "You're going to go through the rest of your life alone, afraid of what fate has in store for you, afraid to reach out for what's within your reach. My God, Cliff, don't you think happiness, even if it lasts only a moment, is worth taking a chance on?"

"If I did, then I wouldn't be telling you goodbye." His face hardened once again and his voice was cold.

"And that's what you're doing? Telling me goodbye?" His nod was her answer, and she turned away, wanting to leave before her tears fell. She got as far as the front door, then paused with her hand on the doorknob, her back to Cliff. "I just want you to know. If you ever decide to take a chance again—if you ever decide to fight the fear that is eating you up inside, you know where to find me. I love you, Cliff.'' With these final words Edie opened the door and ran from his apartment.

In some small section of her mind she hoped he would stop her, hoped he would come running after her and take her in his arms and say he'd been a fool, that he hadn't meant any of the things he'd said.

She got into her car and sat for a moment, hoping the door of his apartment would fly open and he would run out, eyes searching wildly for her. She laughed bitterly at her romantic fantasies. She'd been the fool. She had nobody to blame but herself. He'd made her no promises. If this had been a romance novel he would come after her and they would end up in each other's arms. But this was reality and he wasn't coming after her. He had meant his goodbye.

Cliff stood in the window of his apartment, watching Edie get into her car. He had been deliberately wounding, choosing words to inflict pain, words to drive her away. He sighed tremulously as he watched her pull out of the parking lot and disappear down the street.

Love, what a reckless sort of gamble it all was, he thought as he grabbed his bags and carried them out to his car. Better to leave his heart hardened by Catherine and never take a chance on being hurt again.

Ten

The drive from Kansas City to St. Louis was five hours, but to Cliff it seemed like a ten-day drive of torture. All of nature conspired to make it impossible for him to forget the woman he'd said goodbye to.

The burnished golds and reds of the leaves on the trees reminded him of the highlights in Edie's hair. The browning of the earth with the coming of winter was her eyes, haunting him mile after mile.

Dusk fell, reminding him of how many nights he'd sat at the window in Edie's apartment, watching twilight paint her features with a lovely glow.

Oh, how he wished things could have been different. How he wished he had met Edie years before, when his heart had dared to hope, and dreams had come easily.

It was with enormous relief that he pulled in to the suburban ranch house where his mother had lived with her second husband for the past five years. He saw a flash of movement at the front window, then as he unkinked and got out of the car, his mother burst through the door at a dead run. He'd hardly had a chance to stand up straight before she hit him midsection, hurling herself against him, her arms pulling him into a breath-threatening embrace.

For a long moment he merely stood, returning her hug, enjoying the cinnamon scent of her that evoked memories of his childhood.

"Oh, my boy," she murmured, then pulled back so she could look fully into his face. "I knew eventually you'd come back to all of us." Her dark eyes searched his face lovingly, then she smiled, obviously satisfied with what she saw there. "Your eyes are clear. You've learned to live with your pain." He nodded, smiling fully as his mother reached up and stroked his cheek. "It's a good face, Cliff, now that the anger and bitterness are gone."

"You think if we went inside, you could find a cup of coffee for this good face?" Cliff asked as his mother reluctantly released her grip on him.

"I think I could manage that." She smiled at him and linking arms they walked side by side into the house.

The place was just the same as it had been almost three years earlier when Cliff and Catherine had come for a weekend visit. He went over to the living-room window where a wooden stand held an array of greenery. He reached out and lightly touched the deep purple bloom of an African violet. Catherine had brought the plant to his mother on their last visit here.

"I've never seen a plant that blossoms like that one." His mother spoke softly from behind him. "It's funny that somebody as impatient and selfish as Catherine could choose such a plant."

Cliff nodded. Yes, Catherine had been impatient and selfish . . . impatient with his long hours and needing more and more of him. His mother had warned him before they ever married that Catherine wasn't a good choice for a cop's wife, but Cliff hadn't wanted to hear it. He'd been blinded by Catherine's beauty, enraptured with the fact that she loved him.

"You know, you were right about her all along," he observed. "You warned me and I didn't listen." He turned and smiled at his mother.

She shrugged. "Right, wrong—there is no such thing in a divorce. There's only pain." His mother's eyes were dark with empathy.

Cliff put his arm around his mother's shoulders. "But that's gone now, and I've recently discovered that life goes on."

"Yes, life goes on." She smiled at him warmly, then tugged him into the kitchen. "And the coffee is ready."

"Where's Joe? Isn't he usually home by this time of the evening?" Cliff asked once he and his mother were seated at the kitchen table.

"Not this time of year. With winter just around the corner, Joe stays busy servicing and cleaning furnaces. I become a heating-and-cooling-business widow in the spring and fall of every year." She reached across the table and touched his hand lightly. "Joe will be so happy to see you, Cliff. He's missed your visits."

"I've missed visiting with him, too." As Cliff said the words he realized how true they were. From the moment his mother had married Joe Forrester five years earlier, Cliff and Joe had found an instant rapport that was rare between men. Joe was a quiet, methodical man who valued his marriage, his work and an occasional beer on a Sunday afternoon during the football game. Perhaps the thing Cliff liked most about Joe was the fact that Joe so obviously loved Cliff's mom.

Cliff looked at his mother objectively for the first time since he had arrived. In the five years that she'd been married to Joe, she seemed somehow to have regressed in age. Oh, there was a little more gray intertwined in her dark hair, and several character lines crept stealthily across her forehead, yet she emitted an aura of youth, of happiness. Was that what love did to people? Make their eyes sparkle and their faces glow? Hadn't he once read somewhere that married people lived longer than single people?

Then why, when he thought of Edie and the love he felt for her, did he feel so ancient? "You're happy, aren't you?" he asked his mother suddenly.

"It should be sinful to feel as happy as I'm feeling at this moment," she answered, pausing to sip her coffee, then continued. "Now, if you'd have asked me yesterday, the answer would have been a little different."

"Why?"

"Yesterday there was a piece missing from my life, and that piece was my son."

This time it was Cliff who reached across the table and grabbed his mother's hand. "Why'd we let the distance between us go on so long, Mom? What happened with us?"

Anna Forrester sighed. "Oh, honey, you don't know how many times in the past two years I asked myself that very same question." She looked at him thoughtfully. "When Catherine left, you were so devastated. You hugged your grief tightly to yourself instead of reaching out for the people who loved you. We all backed away, thinking the best thing we could do was give you some time to yourself. But time seemed to deepen your grief and harden your bitterness. When I phoned you, I couldn't stand to hear that in your voice. It got easier and easier not to call." She patted his hand. "I hoped in time you'd come back to us. I don't know what helped you find peace within yourself, but I'm grateful that you've finally come home."

Edie . . . Edie made me find peace within myself, he wanted to answer, but he didn't. What was the point of telling his mother about Edie? He'd turned his back on her, refused to allow her to become a part of his life, so what was there to tell? Why talk about a woman whose eyes mirrored her soul, reflecting a love he found bewildering and more than a little bit frightening?

"Anna, I'm home." The words were punctuated by the opening of the front door.

With a sigh of relief Cliff pulled his thoughts away from Edie and got up from the table to greet his step-father.

Cliff sat on the porch swing in the backyard of his mother's house. He'd been in St. Louis for three days, and Edie was no less on his mind now than she had been when he had driven down from Kansas City.

In fact, seeing his mother and Joe together, seeing the loving comfort they offered each other, the quiet contentment that existed between them only served to remind him that he could have had that with Edie, if he wasn't so damned scared. And yet, today, with the sun shining brightly overhead, and the changing of the seasons evident all around him, the concept of fear seemed inconsequential. Was his fear of the future great enough to sacrifice the love he could have with Edie? He was beginning to wonder.

He'd also begun to realize that when Catherine left him it wasn't so much his grief over the loss of her that had devastated him, it had been the loss of the dream of happily ever after. He'd always assumed he'd marry once and it would be forever. Catherine had stolen that particular dream from him.

"What are you doing out here all by yourself?" his mother asked, coming out of the house and joining him on the swing.

"Oh, just contemplating the complexities of life." He smiled at his own words, remembering when he and Edie had had much the same conversation on the day she had taken him to her magic rock. It had been that same day that Nanny had fallen down the stairs.

He wondered now how the older woman was getting along. It was also on that day that he and Edie had made love for the second time.

"What's the matter, son? Is it Catherine?" his mother asked, making him realize his face had spasmed with pain at thoughts of Edie.

"No, it's not Catherine," he hurriedly assured her. "I've finally made my peace with Catherine and the divorce. I've met someone else." He turned and looked at his mother beseechingly. "And suddenly I'm terribly confused."

"Tell me," she instructed softly. And as they sat gently swinging, with the sun warming their shoulders, Cliff told his mother everything about Edie and Nanny, from the moment he had been assigned the surveillance case to when he'd sent Edie on her way on the day he had left for St. Louis. He held nothing back, telling her of his initial hostility, the anger that had in some crazy way grown into love.

When he was finished, his mother was silent for a long time. When she finally began to talk, her voice was low and laced with the pain of the past.

"Years ago, when your father left us, I worried about how you would adjust. I was so afraid that the scar of his abandonment would be with you forever. I was also worried about myself. How was I ever going to trust a man again? I'd given your father all I had to give and it still wasn't enough to keep him."

"Mom..." Cliff heard the pain and didn't want her to continue remembering the sadness of the past. He also related to what she was saying, having felt exactly the same way.

"No, it's all right." She smiled at him reassuringly, then continued. "Oh, Cliff, I was so happy when you married Catherine, even though I wasn't sure of her. I was pleased that you had risen above your childhood. Now you tell me there is another woman in your life, a woman who is offering you love, and it hurts my heart to know you're running away from her."

"But when do you stop taking chances?" he asked painfully.

"When you're dead."

"How would you feel if something happened tomorrow to Joe and he decided to leave you? Wouldn't you regret giving your heart to him only to have it smashed to bits by some cruel quirk of fate?"

"Let me tell you what I regret. Two months after I started dating Joe, he asked me to marry him and I told him no. For over a year I put him off, afraid to make a commitment to a man ever again. If something happened to Joe tomorrow, the only regret I would have would be that I didn't agree to marry him the first time he asked me and that I wasted a whole year that we could have spent together. Cliff..." Her gaze sought his, holding him with the wisdom that radiated from her darker, older eyes. "Love never has regrets—only those who run from love have regrets." She patted his hand and smiled enigmatically. "Think about it, son." She rose and went back into the house, leaving Cliff alone with his thoughts.

"Thank you for your time, Mrs. Stevenson. I'll be in touch when I've completed reading all the literature,'' Edie said, leading the thin, sour-faced woman to the door.

"Discipline, that's the key to dealing with the elderly. Firm discipline.'' Mildred Stevenson nodded her head in self-righteous wisdom. ''We at Happy Manor believe that's the key.''

"Thank you, I'll keep that in mind.'' Edie smiled pleasantly, then ushered the woman out the door, shut it and leaned against it wearily. Happy Manor, indeed. If Mrs. Stevenson was an indication of the staff, Happy Manor Nursing Home was run by a bunch of pit bulls.

She sighed and flopped down on the sofa, grabbed the list of prospective nursing facilities she'd made and scratched through Happy Manor.

She'd visited three in the past two days, and Mrs. Stevenson had offered to come and discuss the merits of her particular establishment, but so far Edie hadn't been impressed with any of them. She pushed herself off the sofa and moved across the room, sitting at the table and staring at the window. She'd done a lot of this over the past four days since she'd talked to Cliff—sitting and thinking. She found herself going over and over their final conversation in her mind, thinking about what she could have said to him, what she could have done to change his mind. Yet she knew that nothing she could have said or done would have made any difference.

The hardest part for Edie was the loneliness. She'd become accustomed to the apartment being filled with life, but for the past four days the apartment had been filled with only ghosts. Nanny being in the hospital was difficult, but it was Cliff's absence that would always leave a gaping hole in her life.

"Enough," she said aloud. She'd spent too much time dwelling on things that couldn't be changed. In a few hours she had an appointment at Heritage Home, an assisted living facility. In the meantime she wanted to fix herself a sandwich and have a cup of tea.

She'd just finished making herself an avocado and cheese sandwich when a knock sounded on her door. *Probably Rose checking to see if I've had any success in finding a place for Nanny,* Edie thought as she hurried to the door.

She pulled open the door, then immediately slammed it shut, shock riveting through her.

"Edie . . ." Cliff's voice came through the door.

For a moment Edie couldn't answer. Her heart was in her throat, choking off her breath.

"Ma'am, my name is Cliff Marchelli and I'm with the Kansas City Police Department."

His words, so reminiscent of the first time they had met, brought a pain-laced smile to her face. "Yeah, right, and I'm Zsa Zsa Gabor," she returned in a small voice just loud enough for him to hear.

"Edie, can I come in? I need to talk to you."

What was he doing here? What did he want from her? Another fleeting moment without commitment? She couldn't. She couldn't hold him in her arms, feel his skin warm against hers, without wanting more than just a passing minute of his life. "You told me everything I needed to know the other day," she said in a tight voice, steeling her heart against any emotional assault he might make.

"Edie, please, let me in."

She opened the door slowly and allowed him to step inside, then closed it behind him. "My apartment is no longer available for police surveillance, and if that's what you're here for, I'm going to throw you out on your ear." She looked at him defiantly.

Cliff grinned a full, heartfelt smile that made her breath catch once again in her throat. "Actually, this isn't a business call. I'm here for purely personal reasons." He reached out for her hand and took it in his.

Edie jerked her hand free and sat on the sofa. "What do you want, Cliff?" Her voice was more harsh than she intended, reflecting the inner turmoil his touch had caused her. Oh, God, why was he here? Why was he tormenting her with his presence?

"What do I want?" Cliff walked by the kitchen table, pausing to look at her sandwich with a grimace. "I want to know if you're still going to insist on eating stuff like that after we're married?"

Edie stared at him blankly. My God, it had finally happened—the stress she had been under the past couple of days had affected her hearing.

"Edie...I just proposed marriage to you. Would it be too much to ask that I hear your answer?"

She continued to stare blankly at him. "Marry?" Anger suddenly rippled through her. Who did she think he was to waltz in here after breaking her heart and calmly announce he wanted to marry her? "Why on earth would I want to marry you?" She jumped off the sofa, pacing the room in agitation. "You're a pretty poor bet for husband material. You're definitely a Type *A* personality. You have ulcers and no

dreams. You eat junk food and you probably snore."
She glared at him, her anger masking a deeper, more
profound fear. Did she dare hope? He had been so
adamant four days ago about his own desire to remain uninvolved, uncommitted.

"Edie." He took her hands once again in his, and
this time she allowed him to lead her back to the sofa,
where they both sat down. "Ulcers can heal, and I can
always change my eating habits. I don't snore, and I
only need one thing to give me dreams—you."

Edie's anger was suddenly gone, leaving only a
trembling, vulnerable vestige of hope. "Cliff, I don't
understand.... The other day, the things you said..."

He released one of her hands and reached out to
gently touch the side of her face. "The words of a
foolish, frightened man."

"But what made you change your mind?" She
needed to know what had made his change of heart.
She needed to know if she could trust the surety she
saw in his eyes.

"Ah, Edie." He smiled softly. "I think I was a
goner the first time I laid eyes on you." He shook his
head slowly. "I tried fighting it. God knows, I didn't
want to be in love with you. I'd spent the last two years
of my life convincing myself I didn't need love. I work
in one of the most dangerous professions there is, and
four days ago I was spouting off how frightened I was
of taking risks, of being afraid of fate. It wasn't until
this morning, when I woke up and my heart felt so
heavy, like fate had already dealt me a deadly blow,
that I realized it was too late to be afraid. The worst
had already happened. I love you, and no matter how

far I run, no matter how much I deny the fact, it is a fact.''

"Oh, Cliff..." She moved into his arms without hesitation. His arms enfolded her tightly, so tightly she couldn't breathe. But she didn't need to breathe; all she needed was for him to go on holding her forever. Suddenly she couldn't get close enough to him. She kissed his eyes, his forehead, his chin, straining her body against his in joyous release.

"Oh, Edie, I love you," he whispered into her hair. "I want all the fleeting moments you can give me, enough to fill up a lifetime."

"And I love you," Edie breathed tremulously. "And I'd be happy to share my fleeting moments with you." She laughed in delight as he stood and swooped her up in his arms.

"I think it's time we start our lifetime together right now," he said, his voice husky and his eyes gazing at her in that hungry way that made the blood pound and sing in her veins.

"I think you're absolutely right." She wrapped her arms around his neck as he carried her into the bedroom and gently deposited her on the bed.

It was some time later that they lay side by side, talking about their life together.

"We have to have a big, juicy steak at least once a month," Cliff murmured, his breath warm and loving on Edie's neck as they snuggled together on the small bed. "And tacos...once a week we have to make tacos for Nanny."

Edie nodded, her heart so filled she couldn't speak. With Cliff by her side she knew she would make the right decision for Nanny, and together the three of them would turn fleeting moments into golden days of happiness and love.

Epilogue

"Come on, Cliff. We don't want to be late," Edie called into the bedroom.

"I'm coming, I'm coming." Cliff walked out of the bedroom, tucking his white shirt into his charcoal gray slacks. He grinned at Edie, causing her heart to convulse in her chest. God, would she ever get enough of him?

"How do I look?" she asked, reaching up to capture an errant lock of hair and shove it behind her ear.

He walked over to her and gently patted her bulging tummy. "You both look gorgeous."

Edie flushed. She was six months pregnant and this was the first time she'd had to wear one of her maternity dresses. "I look fat," she returned.

Cliff pulled her into his arms and placed a lingering kiss on her lips. "You look loved, which you are.

Now, let's get out of here or we'll be late, and it's not every day Nanny is chosen as May Queen.''

Within minutes they were in the car on their way to the spring festivities at Heritage Home, the place where Nanny had been living for the past seven months. Edie settled back in the car seat and contemplated those seven months.

She had finally decided on Heritage Home for Nanny after visiting the assisted living facilities. She'd been impressed by the homey surroundings and the fact that the elderly people in care there were encouraged to continue pursuing hobbies and interests. And since being placed there, Nanny had thrived. Although she had to be reintroduced to her friends each day, and twice she had orchestrated escape plans that were discovered in the nick of time, she seemed happy.

Happiness seemed to be in abundance these days. Edie had never known so much could exist in her life. She gazed over at Cliff, who was responsible for so much of the joy in her life. Poor Catherine, she would never realize what she'd walked out on, for Cliff was a loving, caring, passionate husband. Edie placed a hand on her stomach, knowing he would make a wonderful father, as well.

"You'd better quit looking at me like that or we'll never make it to Heritage Home," Cliff warned her. "I'll have to find a motel and take advantage of your body."

Edie laughed and rubbed her stomach again. "I think it's too late for that."

He wheeled the car into the parking lot of the brick, one-story building where Nanny resided. The parking lot was filled, and the grounds were decorated with spring flowers and lawn chairs, balloons and crepe paper. They got out of the car and approached the festivities, greeting people they had come to know over the past several months.

"Oh, Cliff, look." Edie pointed to a lounge chair where Nanny sat dozing, a paper crown askew on her head.

"Looks like the May Queen is taking her royal nap," Cliff said as they approached Nanny.

Edie leaned over and brushed a strand of Nanny's white hair away from her eyes, then kissed her cheek softly. Nanny's eyes fluttered open and she smiled brightly. "Oh, I'm so glad you came today. All my friends are here and we're having a lovely tea party."

"We wouldn't have missed it for the world," Edie exclaimed.

Nanny's eyes darkened as she caught sight of Cliff. "Oh, I see you brought him with you again. Doesn't he have a home?"

"Don't you remember, Nanny? This is my husband, Cliff. Remember you came to our wedding?" Edie explained patiently.

Nanny's brow wrinkled in thought. "No...no, I don't remember a wedding." Her eyes widened as she noticed Edie's protruding stomach. "Did he do that?" She reached out and cuffed Cliff on the side of the head. "You'd better take care of my Edie. She's something special."

Cliff smiled. "I intend to take care of her for the rest of my life." He leaned down and gave Nanny a kiss on her cheek. "And you're pretty special, too."

Nanny looked at him for a long moment. "Maybe you'll do, after all," she said, then promptly closed her eyes.

* * * * *

COMING NEXT MONTH

TRIPLE TREAT
Barbara Boswell

Tyler Tremaine was footloose and fancy-free until he met his neighbour Carrie Wilcox and her three toddling triplets!

YESTERDAY'S HERO
Debbie Macomber

Leah Talmadge and Cain Hawkins both desperately wanted to travel to the Diamantina Islands, but the Governor denied permission for two unmarried people to live together; there was only one solution—marriage!

PRIDE AND PROMISES
BJ James

Ross McLachlan and Antonia Russell, the country doctor and the glamorous movie star, thanks to a twist of fate and a friend's matchmaking they were in a small plane together heading into a storm…

COMING NEXT MONTH

MONTANA SKY
Jackie Merritt

Jennifer Auburn had moved to the city, but she hadn't known what she was missing back home on her father's Montana ranch. For instance, there was rugged Reno Banning who made jeans look positively sinful...

THE WRANGLER AND THE RICH GIRL
Joan Johnston

Garth Whitelaw was determined that he wasn't going to fall victim to love as his brothers and sister had. Even a rich, beautiful, loving innocent couldn't tempt him! Could she?

HIGH SPIRITS
Rita Rainville

Marcy O'Bannon was ghost hunting, much to cop Nick Stoner's irritation. That meant she was wandering around deserted houses at all hours of the day...and night! She needed a keeper!

COMING NEXT MONTH FROM

Silhouette

Sensation

*romance with a special mix of
suspense, glamour and drama*

DANGEROUS STRANGER Naomi Horton
LIGHTNING STRIKES Kathleen Korbel
SEIZE THE MOMENT Ann Major
DESPERATE MEASURES Paula Detmer Riggs

Special Edition

*longer, satisfying romances with
mature heroines and lots of emotion*

SWEET BURNING Sandi Shane
LORD OF THE DESERT Barbara Faith
THE GAME OF LOVE Heather Graham Pozzessere
DEVIL'S NIGHT Jennifer Greene
THE SIMPLE TRUTH Sandy Steen
THE NAME OF THE GAME Nora Roberts